THE G

Susan Hillmore is a painter and novelist, living in Gloucestershire. She studied Fine Art at Camberwell School of Art. *The Greenhouse* was shortlisted for the *Sunday Express* Book of the Year award. She is also the author of *Malaria*, her second novel, published in 2000.

ALSO BY SUSAN HILLMORE

Malaria

Susan Hillmore

THE GREENHOUSE

V

VINTAGE

Published by Vintage 2000

2 4 6 8 10 9 7 5 3

Copyright © Susan Hillmore 1988

The right of Susan Hillmore to be identified as the author of
this work has been asserted by her in accordance with the
Copyright, Designs and Patents Act, 1988

First published in Great Britain in 1988 by
Collins Harvill

Vintage
Random House, 20 Vauxhall Bridge Road,
London SW1V 2SA

Random House Australia (Pty) Limited
20 Alfred Street, Milsons Point, Sydney
New South Wales 2061, Australia

Random House New Zealand Limited
18 Poland Road, Glenfield,
Auckland 10, New Zealand

Random House (Pty) Limited
Endulini, 5A Jubilee Road, Parktown 2193,
South Africa

The Random House Group Limited Reg. No. 954009
www.randomhouse.co.uk

A CIP catalogue record for this book
is available from the British Library

ISBN 0 09 928318 2

Papers used by Random House are natural, recyclable
products made from wood grown in sustainable forests.
The manufacturing processes conform to the environ-
mental regulations of the country of origin

Printed and bound in Great Britain by
Cox & Wyman Limited, Reading, Berkshire

To Peter

THE MASSIVE SKELETON of the empty Greenhouse stood alone on a cold November night. Outside, dry umbrellas of hemlock quaked as a sharp East wind left its quarter and travelled towards the Greenhouse, where it recoiled as it cut itself on some broken glass. A hunting fox stopped in his tracks, one paw raised motionless, ears pricked, nose high testing the air. The mist thickened into a fog that swallowed up the charcoal smudges of the landscape. A blackbird called out a warning at the progress of the fox. One by one the night sentries took up the alarm. The fox crouched in his own stillness, got up and began to stalk his prey. The birds went quiet. The Greenhouse stood closed to the night. Its glass eyes reflected the solid whiteness of the fog where it lay at the bottom of the bank, straining to rise, only to fall confused amongst the undergrowth before being crushed by the cold night air. The stifled death-scream of a hare sounded from the meadow. A thin layer of ice began to form across the surface of the water tank outside. The Greenhouse listened until the dripping tap froze, cracking and contracting with pain as it remembered its past.

*

The Greenhouse was a magnificent structure. It stood with its back against a wall and rose to more than three times the height of a man. Inside, tall fluted, cast-iron columns decorated with acanthus leaves stretched up to its glass, where they were reflected upwards until they joined the sky to the earth. Its floor was feathered with ochre and cream tiles. The façade was divided by six square limestone pillars, their capitals carved on all four corners with scrolls, supporting a roof of intricately fretted wood and ironwork, which at its highest point was ornamented by finials that peaked into the heavens. Between each pillar stood a tall arched window whose glass was set between the finest wood astragals. The lightness and symmetry of the Greenhouse's proportions created an illusion of fragility which disguised its extraordinary strength in face of any extremity of the weather. By day it would blaze like a multi-faceted precious stone; at dusk it would glow, soft as a pearl. In frost or mist it floated high on its bank as if at the water's edge.

To the Greenhouse time was measured by the passing of the seasons; by the early flowering of the Lenten rose; the flushing of the trees in Spring; white lilac spiked against dark yew; warm Summer evenings of shadows lengthening over petal-strewn grass; ripeness, followed by ferment and decay.

There had been Summers of light so intense that gardeners came with ladders and tin buckets of limewash to paint each glass eye of the Greenhouse, so that it stood blind to the outside world under a pale Summer cloud. There had been days of damping, syringing and chemical

8

spraying against the unseen spores of destruction. The air within the Greenhouse was always carefully controlled so that it might not be too hot or too cold, too wet or too dry. There was the annual painful scrubbing of every inch of its interior with paraffin and soft soap, followed by the application of a dreadful creamy wash of skimmed milk, lime and sulphur painted on to the interior of its retaining wall. Gardeners had worked at the endless preparation of sterile soils, at the extermination of insects which, if permitted to fertilize an orchid, would cause it to blush red and collapse its petals in a day. Looking down on the orchid, tuberose, camellia and musk, and being filled with their scent, the Greenhouse swelled with a bubble of pride in those first seasons of its existence.

Winters had been warm. Huge cast-iron heating pipes ran the length of the Greenhouse to the boiler housed behind its wall, which was fuelled with coke day and night to maintain the temperatures necessary for the growth of rare tropical plants.

Russet woodmice squeezed their nut-filled bellies through the gap where the pipes entered the Greenhouse and lay somnolent in straw until hunger woke them; then they scuttered up to the staging and were caught in the dark by the spring of a trap. The Greenhouse watched the pleasure that the gardeners took in their capture. They nailed each of those dead mice to a batten under a bench, and after the Winter a tally was taken and money changed hands. They pulled the shrivelled creatures from where they were pinned and threw them into a bucket. Stiff-limbed, toes clenched, they lay in a pile waiting with the

Winter's other debris to be taken away for incineration.

As the years passed the gardeners left. The boiler stood empty, its fuel door hanging open; clinker and ashes still lay on the iron grille inside. The old hods, half-full of fuel, rusted to the colour of the broken rhubarb-forcing pots that were stacked outside.

The woodwork was still painted each year by a man from the nearby village, and broken or slipped panes of glass were set back in place. The old hard putty that had lifted and cracked was scraped away and the smell of linseed oil would temporarily drown the scent of the season. The wooden staging that had supported the orchids, the hotbeds that had once held pineapples, the huge tubs for oranges, peaches and nectarines were empty. There were still pots of lilies, and when they flowered they reminded the Greenhouse of its exotic past.

The fox returned to his earth, still moving his head from side to side, testing the wind, listening, before taking a well-worn track back through the sedge by the stream. Outside, the Greenhouse felt the onset of Winter in the brittle silk-wrapped chrysalis of a butterfly pressed against its cold glass. As the night passed, the fog condensed and froze on the surface of all that it touched. The Greenhouse slipped into hibernation until Spring.

The Greenhouse looked out over its domain. Immediately in front of it the rough unmown Spring grass was sharp green against the bluer leaves of the pheasant's-eye narcissi, which at this hour turned their heads away from the Greenhouse to face the South and the sun. This grass extended the entire length of a raised level bank, interrupted by a flight of stone steps down to the lawns below, where the grass was duller in colour, scattered with daisies, blue speedwell and a recent fall of glittering hailstones. To the East, at the far end of the boundary wall against which the Greenhouse stood, ran a narrow, noisy stream. In its water lived thin brown trout that swam heads against the flow, rising from time to time to the surface in pursuit of the first hatch of fly that would fatten them. Beyond the far bank of the stream stretched the water meadows, ending in a dense line of trees. From the shade of the wood emerged a wide ribbon of track, planted on either side with pale-leaved limes. It crossed the stream over a flat single-arched bridge, built of the same stone as the Greenhouse wall and the house, then cut across the lawns and merged with the gravel in front of the house before leading off to the farmyard that lay at the back. The yard was not visible to the Greenhouse for the massive bulk of the house obscured its view.

The house lay to the West of the Greenhouse, casting a long shadow at sunset that stretched across the lawns but never quite reached the rising ground on which the Greenhouse stood.

The Greenhouse regretted that it should never see the full front of the house. It could see obliquely along the flat stone face and just observe which windows were open and which were shuttered, the comings and goings to the front door, but no-one came or went. Even Vanessa, now alone, had used the back door since the war began and her brother Hugo left.

The Greenhouse regarded as within its territory part of the area behind the house leading to the yard. There the farmer made his cider and kept his tractor, the farmer's wife reared her hens and rabbits in cages for the table. The Greenhouse knew from the acrid smell of pigswill and fermenting cider apples that the yard was a dusty hard-baked place where half-starved kittens fought with rats for food in sunless sheds among the rusting ploughshares. Beyond the house stood the church and its tower with the long silent bell and running-fox weather vane. In the churchyard stood a cedar, only its topmost portion visible above the roof of the house, its branches stretched, dark-fingered and still, against a clearing sky.

For some years the Greenhouse had seen the countryside deserted by all the young men and women who had gone away to the war. A vicar still came to the church from time to time and the Greenhouse watched as a congregation composed of women, children, the farmer, his wife and a handful of those who worked the land filed past the low churchyard wall. Vanessa did not attend; her self-imposed isolation prevented her. She was like the sole remaining member of a contemplative order.

The Greenhouse had always felt a particular bond be-tween itself and Vanessa. On Vanessa the Greenhouse was dependent. Without her care it would decay. Without her presence it would be alone.

Her childhood had taught her to deal with solitude. From the day of her birth Vanessa's father had been unable to accept that his daughter was a cripple, different from other children. While she lay in her cot or was wheeled out in her pram he could pretend that she was the same as other babies. She was always swaddled by her mother or her nurse, her legs tied fast to one another. Her smiles and cries were like those of any child. She was pretty and alert. When brought to him she was always dressed in a long gown that stretched well below her toes.

Her deformity remained invisible to him until one warm day when he was sitting out on the lawn having breakfast with her mother. Vanessa had been left in her pram lightly wrapped beside them. She woke. The Greenhouse watched her twist and squirm in the pram until she was able to sit up and look towards her parents. She smiled in their direction and fell back. Again the child struggled to sit up, twisting her tiny body with all the strength she had. The shawl with which she had been covered came free and she started to play with it, pushing her fingers through its lacy holes.

Her father turned the page of his newspaper. Her mother poured out another cup of tea and glanced over at Vanessa, who once again had managed to sit up. She picked up the small glass bell that was used to summon the nurse; its ring delighted the child. No-one noticed when the shawl finally fell on to the grass. Vanessa's mother returned to her tea and sipped. A blackbird twittered an alarm call from the roof the Greenhouse. Vanessa hung over the side of the pram, looked down at the lost shawl and began to cry. She lay back and in a rage kicked her naked legs in the air until they were free. Her father got up, still carrying the newspaper, and looked down at the red-faced, screaming infant. One of her feet was beating against the side of the pram; the other, deformed and twisted, was flexing backwards and forwards like the claw of a helpless crab. He tore the paper apart, dropped it and strode away towards the house. Moments later the nurse arrived and removed the child, who was now lying covered by the shawl in the arms of her mother. The newspaper drifted in crackling chaos across the lawn.

Vanessa began to learn to walk. A leg iron was fitted for the first time, attached to an ugly brown boot. Her father insisted that she should always be dressed in frocks whose hems touched the ground, despite the fact that they made walking almost impossible. He dictated that no other child should ever be admitted to the grounds. Her mother acquiesced.

The Greenhouse watched the small child, hardly able to walk, as she pulled herself up its steps, pushed open its doors and, by clinging on to its frame, stood erect. Her wide face beamed at what she saw inside. Flowers and fruits that even her fertile imagination had been unable to invent hid under leaves that were shinier than the hard false wings of a beetle's back in the sun. A ripe orange hanging from a low branch attracted her. She attempted to run to it, as if continuous movement would help her keep her balance, and she fell hard on the tiled floor. She lay there beating her splayed palms on the ground in frustration before turning herself to sit up and examine her skinned knee. It was then that the child's physical constraints seemed to the Greenhouse to be very like its own. It too was limited, tied to the wall and, like Vanessa, was to spend its entire existence in the same place. For her part she continued to walk unevenly but with determination, refusing to accept her physical confinement.

Vanessa's father was kind to her; he grew to love her more as the years passed. She was fascinated by his great Greenhouse. He encouraged her and taught her all that he knew, for one day she would be the inheritor of his passion. She followed her father everywhere. He tried mastering his irritation at her awkward lurching gait, and she would place only her toe down on any hard surface so that the leg iron never struck the ground, in order not to vex him. But publicly her father could not admit to the burden of his crippled daughter, so Vanessa was educated on her own by a series of resident tutors. One after another they left, either unable to remain for long in that remote country house, or unsettled by the harsh treatment of the child.

Vanessa's mother appeared to show no concern for her daughter. Throughout the years of her marriage she fluctuated between robust health and long periods of frailty, during which the doctor would call at the house daily and sometimes return at night.

*

Both her brothers had been killed during The Great War. The shock and grief of their successive deaths was believed to account for her debility. The Greenhouse often watched her ride out side-saddle on a fine chestnut hack. She was smartly dressed in a hat and dun drill habit and always followed by a groom. She would gallop away across the fields only to return in a state of collapse. Her gelding would be led away to the yard and she would be helped into the house supported by two maids. After this would come weeks of inactivity. No-one would visit. The shutters of the rooms upstairs would be part-closed, as if a death had taken place. Vanessa had a pony but the Greenhouse did not ever see mother and child ride out together.

One morning when the frost was sharp and the air froze breath, the Greenhouse heard the quarrelling of a pack of hounds followed by the dull noise of hooves coming through the wood. Rider after rider trotted out and along the track between the avenue of limes. They assembled in front of the house on the gravel. The animals twisted and turned, crushing the stones, quarter against quarter, nostrils breathing out a fog of swirling vapour. Coupled hounds held tight together were kept to one side of the front door, out of which Vanessa's mother emerged followed by servants carrying trays. The Greenhouse watched as white-starched cotton threaded its way through a turmoil of horseflesh. The smell of animal and man softened the morning air. Out of the yard came Vanessa mounted on her well-mannered pony, head high, hair netted under her black hat, perfect white stock set with a pearl pin. She joined the group.

Vanessa's mother mounted her hunter, which was double-bridled and clipped trace-high. She reined it in, it passaged sideways against Vanessa's pony and she turned in the saddle to look down upon her daughter. She raised her crop, pointed it at Vanessa and beckoned her to leave the meet. Shamefaced, Vanessa turned away, cheeks burning so red that she might have been blooded.

As steadily as they had all arrived they left; the kennel huntsman, the first and second whippers-in, and the carrier of two fox terriers. The rest of the field followed. Vanessa returned dejectedly to the yard. Throughout that morning the Greenhouse listened to the hue and cry.

When Vanessa was fourteen years old Hugo was born, perfect, a boy. Her father was ecstatic. He had been burdened for so many years with the recrimination of his own genes, and had tried to compensate with the perfection of the rare tropical plants that he nurtured inside the Greenhouse. With the fulfilment of all that he had ever desired he came to neglect the Greenhouse and his daughter.

The boy was baptized in the church and it seemed to Vanessa that the entire world had been invited. She had never in her life seen another child set foot on the lawns of the house, but on this day it was as if every child for hundreds of miles about had been gathered together for the christening party.

No-one noticed Vanessa. No-one knew Vanessa. She moved between the clusters of relatives and friends, hovered tentatively on the edge of the throng, only to be ignored. She wanted to be a part of this gathering. She started to intrude more forcibly, and lurched forward into the centre of an animated crowd of women who were standing around her mother admiring Hugo, so pale and unreal in his long silk robe. She spoke out loud and was instantly reprimanded for her bad manners in interrupting the conversation. She retreated, stinging with pain, blinking hard in an effort to keep back her tears. But like a moth attracted to a bright light she drove herself into the face of another damaging confrontation.

She joined a group which included a girl of about her own age. She grabbed her hand and asked her to come with her to see her father's pride, his great Greenhouse. The girl followed for a few paces, but noticed the strange way that her companion walked, and felt the uneven pull on her arm. Then, exhibiting the instinctive mistrust that children have for anything or anyone that does not conform to their notion of normal, she pulled away from Vanessa to return to her mother's side. Vanessa, unconscious of the reason for her rejection, approached one child after another in her search for a companion. She failed, and with damaged wings limped away from the party to the Greenhouse, where alone in uncomprehending misery she hid until the light and the people had left the lawns.

Six years after Hugo's birth Vanessa's father was invited to join a botanical expedition to South-east Asia. His orchids were admired by many enthusiastic collectors, and although he was now old, he set off on the long sea voyage. During the months that he was away Vanessa was free to spend more time with her brother. He provided her with the companionship and play that her own childhood had lacked. Despite their difference in age they would spend every possible hour together in the meadows, the garden and the Greenhouse.

At dusk every window of the house would glow, casting rectangles of light on to the gravel. Vanessa and Hugo would come out into the dark. Then, suddenly illuminated like fireflies, they would dart through the light and run down to the stream. The Greenhouse would watch them as they sat, pulling at hunks of bread or whatever Hugo had been able to steal from the kitchen. They would take up their hidden rods from the reeds, weight worms on their hooks and, standing quite still on the bank, waiting, listening for the sound of a rising fish, cast for trout. Vanessa would put her finger in her mouth and pull at the inside of her cheek to imitate the plop of the fish. Enraged, Hugo would throw down his rod and attack his grown-up sister for her silliness, threatening to push her into the stream and not to rescue her, taunting her that her leg iron would rust and she would never escape but would have to live with the trout amongst the weeds and the caddis-fly lava, surrounded by water rats and beetles and hatching dragonfly nymphs. They would laugh and finish the food, and speculate in the dark as to the size of the fish they would catch.

*

Months passed and intermittently letters arrived in batches from their father, containing vivid descriptions of the life of the rain forests, of his expeditions up rivers and creeks, of how monkeys were trained to run up tall trees to collect plant specimens, of elephants and natives and the exotic life in the cities. Together they would sit inside his Greenhouse and Vanessa would read and reread to Hugo these stories of the East.

On the day that the hearse arrived, pulled by a pair of black Dutch horses, Vanessa stood beside her mother in front of the house, both women dressed in black. Hugo was overcome with excitement and danced on the gravel in his belief that his father had finally come home. The silver decorations on the bridles and harness tinkled and glittered and stung in the light. Hugo was restrained by Vanessa as the coffin was unloaded and carried into the house. Their father had died of a fever on the return sea crossing, and after his funeral in the church Vanessa's mother collapsed in grief. She retreated to the upstairs rooms of the house and refused to see anyone. Hugo was sent away to school. Vanessa took over the management of the house and the Greenhouse. The orchids were sold and nothing replaced them. Several gardeners were sacked and flowers were no longer taken to the house. One by one the staff left for more rewarding jobs and Vanessa remained alone to look after her mother.

Several years passed. War came. On hearing that Hugo had enlisted in the Army, his mother readily convinced herself that the boy would be killed. This plunged her into such extreme melancholia that she refused to eat and, not long after, died. For months afterwards Vanessa's guilt at her failure to rouse her mother from her depression lent her the look of a penitent. She would walk with hunched shoulders and bowed head, as morbid as the sick woman who had lingered for so long upstairs.

Vanessa's father had left a will dividing his children's inheritance equally. This was surprising, for it was expected that Hugo should inherit everything. However, he had considered that his daughter's deformity made her chances of marriage negligible, and she needed some protection from the outside world.

The Greenhouse had to change; it was no longer possible to maintain it at its past temperatures in the face of austerity. All heating ceased. The last gardener left and Vanessa was alone. She had not married. Now, at forty, the possibility was remote. The danger of her leaving the Greenhouse was past. Vanessa was bound to the Greenhouse, locked into these few acres of land by circumstances and love. For Vanessa loved the Greenhouse and the Greenhouse loved Vanessa. To her it was enchanted, separate from the world, the secret garden of her childhood, the place where anything was possible. The Greenhouse saw her dependence on it, recognized her as its willing captive and was content.

*

Vanessa was inside the Greenhouse, digging the long earth trenches that lay beneath its south wall, on either side of its doors. She was preparing the ground for vines, eight young plants, slender and straight. It was hot now inside the glass but Vanessa continued to work, scattering and forking in the dried blood that she had collected from the farmer after he had killed his pig. This would feed the vines, providing all the elements necessary for their survival. The stench of the blood repelled her and the screams of the pig when it was caught for slaughter distressed her, but it was only on dried blood that the grapes would flourish.

A breeze blew through the open doors and she stood up, running her hand across her forehead. Her blue summer dress clung to her. She narrowed her eyes as she looked directly into the sun towards the track, to where a movement beneath the limes had caught her attention. Vanessa squinted harder. The shadow of a figure cut between the trees. It halted, hiding behind one of them before crossing the grass and vanishing in the direction of the churchyard. Vanessa, uneasy at the appearance of a stranger, returned to her work, looking out hesitantly from time to time, as if she sensed that she was being watched.

The Greenhouse had seen the furtive figure several times before. He would approach from the direction of the village; linger along the track, merge with the background and then, as today, break cover before hiding in the churchyard. At dusk the same man would prowl around the far end of the house until concealed by dark.

Meg, the farmer's sheepdog who was chained at night to a wooden barrel in the yard, would bark ferociously at the intruder, to be thanked for her vigilance by a curse from the farmer, after which she would retreat into her barrel and growl softly at the night.

One evening the man had come closer. He had crept out from the yard and edged cautiously to within a few feet of the Greenhouse until he was just able to see the front of the house. Vanessa was inside. He stood as still as the predatory fox on first scent of its unwitting prey, his back pressed against the Greenhouse wall. A primitive ill will emanated from him; the smell of decay spoiled the fresh evening air. The setting sun began to lengthen his shadow, and drew it inch by inch along the grass bank until it met the foundations of the Greenhouse. The dark silhouette moved stealthily up its ribs and panes until the moment before the sun fell behind the cedar, when it entered the Greenhouse and lingered inside until the coloured sky took all definition from the landscape and smothered it with dusk.

With another hesitant glance outside, Vanessa returned to her work, planting and treading in the soil around the roots of the vines. Beside each she placed a bamboo stick to which she carefully tied the stem for support. Above them she stretched wires to run horizontally along the length of the Greenhouse and attached metal labels naming each variety of grape she was planting.

The figure reappeared in the churchyard, moving between the yew trees and the gravestones. The Greenhouse feared that he had caught sight of the blue of Vanessa's dress behind the reflected brilliance of the glass. It contorted its panes in a vain attempt to blind the figure, to conceal its occupant. It failed.

A huge grey cloud swelled in the sky, bulging like yeast-filled dough; it consumed the blue and obliterated the sun. A shrivelled memory of Winter came to the Greenhouse as a North wind got up behind its back, funnelling over its roof to cross the lawns. Hailstones cut down with such ferocity that Vanessa retreated further into the Greenhouse, as if there she would find more protection.

The clouds left as suddenly as they had arrived. The sun shone through, new and brilliant. Only the trees at the end of the water meadows remained inky black. Small gusts of wind shivered the surface of the stream.

The man climbed over the wall and started to walk across the lawn towards the open glass doors of the Greenhouse. The sunlight had grown stronger. No shadow was cast in the glare. Nothing in the landscape had any definition, only the dark bulk of the man swelling as he came closer. His overcoat was spattered with mud and stalks of straw. His skin was foreign, sallow, his hair unkempt and curiously streaked with red where it had been bleached by the sun. Vanessa raised her fork and then thrust it to the full length of its prongs down into the trench. Supporting herself on the handle she waited uneasily. The man reached the boundary between the lawn and the long grass. He stopped. The Greenhouse glass shone full on his face. He had the luminous empty eyes of a wild creature startled by light. Abruptly, he turned away and dropped his head down into the collar of his overcoat, hiding his face as he passed the length of the Greenhouse in the direction of the stream. There he slowed his pace as he continued along its bank until he reached the lime trees. He cast one last glance back over his shoulder and was then visible only intermittently between their trunks until he vanished into the woods.

The Greenhouse saw that Vanessa had been frightened. She stood looking disturbed in the direction of the trees, still gripping the fork. Then she moved forward towards the doors and out on to the steps, as if to be quite sure that he had gone. Outside she stumbled on a loose stone; it fell to the ground, tearing the head off a narcissus. The flower fell like a dead sun. Its fiery centre and white petals rested on the sharp blades of the grass below.

For the remainder of the afternoon Vanessa continued to plant the vines. Shafts of sunlight from the West filled the side of the Greenhouse, patterning its ochre tiles. In the shadow of the elm tree the farmer's wife scattered corn for her hens. The sun set behind the cedar. The rooks coiled wickedly into the air and circled above the church tower before settling finally to roost.

Vanessa propped the fork against one of the iron columns. She took a brush and swept up the earth and dried blood that had fallen on the floor, releasing their smell into the night air. Then after one last look at the vines, she left. The Greenhouse watched as a single light showed through a window in the house before its shutters were closed, blacking out the night.

The Greenhouse hung on its wall looking down at its new vines. It thought of the man who had disturbed the afternoon and felt again his shadow on its frame. It searched the dark for any sign of his return. There was no moon. The Greenhouse imagined that he hid in the depths of the shadows, feared that it saw him everywhere. It was disturbed by the rattle of a cock pheasant. Then quiet. All that could be heard was the tap's steady drip into the water tank outside. There was no wind. The massive black shadow of the house stood in relief against the sky. The suffocating silence closed about the Greenhouse and the threatening dark seemed to seep in under its doors.

A scream. The murderous cry of a vixen? An owl slaughtering its prey? The unknown sound reverberated through the Greenhouse. White piercing noise sliced through the night. A human cry – terrible human pain – then silence. The Greenhouse waited, felt its own stillness like caught breath. The shock palpitated through its interior. It stood helpless, its iron ties bolting it to the wall.

Lights came on in the house, the sound of muffled activity from within. What could have been a fox leapt over the low churchyard wall. Seconds thudded one upon another. The tap dripped into the water tank. The house went black. The front door opened, grinding the rust from its hinges, releasing a phantom. A figure in a white nightgown ran limping across the grass towards the stream. With all its frame the Greenhouse wanted to cry out to Vanessa to stop. Then, as if she had lost her bearings, she turned and made for the Greenhouse.

The Greenhouse was filled with relief that she had come but dismayed to feel her rapid shallow breath against its glass. Closing the doors behind her she pulled at one of the bamboo canes that supported the new vines and rammed it between the latch and its hold. She shook the doors violently, satisfied herself that they were secure, fumbled her way to one corner, knocking over the fork before reaching a metal chair that stood in one corner. This she dragged screeching against the tiles into the centre of the floor. She positioned it in front of the doors and sat down. The Greenhouse watched as she kept tugging at the ends of her shawl, thrusting her clenched fists down into her lap. She rocked backwards and forwards, mesmerized by despair. The leg iron with its boot stuck out from beneath the hem of her thin white nightgown. The other foot was naked. With her head lolled back and her pupils dilated she lay, like a wide-eyed cadaver, staring through the glass into the night.

As it watched over Vanessa the Greenhouse realized that what had leapt the churchyard wall was not a fox but a man. It strained to see whether there was any further sign of him between the lime trees or around the perimeter of its territory, but the dark was still tight at the margins of the house and only the bats penetrated the imprisoning gloom. The Greenhouse was engulfed by one single

27

monstrous thought. The smell of the man saturated the air with the putrid stench of festering lily bulbs. The Greenhouse looked down on the bruised and violated spectre that was locked within and tried to retain its warmth for her as the night passed and the cold air outside forced itself against the glass.

Vanessa stayed in the Greenhouse for the rest of the night. She appeared not to sleep. The rocking stopped. She just sat there in the middle of the Greenhouse, flanked by two iron pillars, her back to the wall.

A band of light began to show across the water meadows on the other side of the stream. The Greenhouse and Vanessa were coloured by it as if made of some uniform substance. Flesh, wood, metal, stone and glass were indistinguishable until the sun rose. They separated in its warmth. Blood stood in Vanessa's arteries, and veins pulsed in her temples and on the backs of her hands as milky sap rose in the vines. A tortoiseshell butterfly fluttered its wings. Vanessa got to her feet, walked unsteadily to the doors, released the bamboo stick and carefully replaced it in the earth.

She was entirely pale save for a dark stain on her night-gown. The Greenhouse recognized the smell and associated it with the aftermath of terror. It was blood, dried blood. Like the blood taken forcibly at the death of a pig to feed the vines, and the blood carried on the night wind when the fox made a kill. But this blood was different for it was Vanessa's blood, spilt by the man.

Vanessa left, closing the Greenhouse. She walked through the long grass, down the bank to the lawn and on

28

through the open door of the house. Pulling it shut behind her she imprisoned herself within its walls. The Greenhouse heard the sound of the bolts being shot. It was afraid for Vanessa, and afraid for itself, that it might never see her again. She could wither away in that shuttered gloom with no-one to attend to her, just as the Greenhouse's plants would die without care, light and water. The Greenhouse was desolate. The daylight intensified, heating its interior intolerably, simmering the air until it boiled and exploded with terrifying thoughts. Drops of condensation fell to the floor and sizzled in the dust before evaporating. Cankers seemed to burst and fester within as all through the day the Greenhouse waited for Vanessa. Martins darted about the eaves of the house searching for their decayed mud nests, alternating harsh black and white against the stone before turning abruptly upwards into the clear sky. The Greenhouse longed for its doors to be opened, to release the terrors that filled it. It strained for a sound of life from the house, fearing that Vanessa was dead, but, however hard it tried to listen, it was constantly thwarted by the noise of squabbling hedge sparrows and tits. Wood and iron creaked under the strain of the ever-rising temperature and a slow-worm rustled under some dry leaves. The tap outside no longer dripped but hissed out a scant issue of water that bubbled through the drain at the bottom of the overflowing tank. Vanessa did not come. The vines were wilting for lack of water; the Greenhouse was suffocating for lack of ventilation. As midday arrived and the sun shone full from the South the Greenhouse finally slumped down against its wall, resting hard on its supports. The light was now so intense that it was blinded. The flowers turned away.

The church clock striking six woke the Greenhouse from its arid trance. The rooks were performing their evening ritual. The low rays of the sun reflected off every raindrop's smear and every particle of winter dirt that still clung to the outside of the Greenhouse's panes and it could hardly · see out from behind the misty haze. The sun passed behind the cedar and the Greenhouse saw that Vanessa was standing on the bridge, a basket over her arm, gazing down at the water. She seemed unreal. The Greenhouse thought that its fragmented dim vision of her was a tormenting dream. It longed to be able to close all its eyes but was condemned not to. She was dressed entirely in black. Her face was haunted and pale. Only her hair showed any colour as it reddened in the setting sun. The frail and isolated figure of Vanessa lifted her head and turned to the Greenhouse; she stared blankly at it for some time, then slowly began to move away from the bridge and cross the lawn to the long grass where she stopped to pick handfuls of narcissi, piling them loosely into the basket, zigzagging closer and closer until she came to the steps. The Greenhouse looked directly at the taut white-faced creature that stood in front of it: grey eyes darting defensively from side to side, head erect, neck stiff with tension, hands quivering as they touched the glass in its doors before opening them wide. She carried in the flowers and placed them on the chair that she had occupied the night before. The Greenhouse emptied its doubt and fear into the evening air and took in the fresh new scent of the narcissi. Mechanically

Vanessa collected water from the tank, turning off the tap as far as she could. She watered the vines, heaped the blooms into a bucket and left.

From that moment on it was as if the misery and terror of the previous night had been forgotten by Vanessa. Her attention turned to the care of the plants within the Greenhouse. She did not thrive as they grew but strangely fattened and began to sicken. She was distant. Her moods changed as frequently as the colour of the woods beyond the water meadows that the weather might turn from a misty remote blue to stark black. Occasionally sunlight would catch the trees and wash them so pale that they almost disappeared against the sky. Vanessa too, her skin devoid of colour, would seem to evaporate against the glass. The Greenhouse again doubted whether it really was Vanessa who worked and sat within it or whether it was a trace, a phantom of her former self. But the Greenhouse could not survive without her and it could not let her go, so it lived with this ghost that it loved and tried to devise ways of keeping it within its glass for ever.

From June until October lilies flowered in their pots. Simple white waxed madonnas gave way to exotic golden rayed auratum, so like orchids that the Greenhouse, dreaming in their scent, could believe that its past hothouse glory was again present.

Outside, roses and woodbine scrambled up the wall,

stonecrop in its crevices. Yellow kingcups and flags flourished along the margins of the stream. Swallows skimmed the grass for insects in the evenings and wood pigeons burbled on hot afternoons.

Vanessa seemed to have withdrawn completely from the house and the garden and spent much of her time just sitting on the metal chair within the confines of the Greenhouse, her eyes searching for the return of the man, as if he still lurked out there in the landscape, as if, like the fox in his earth, he was hiding until dark, waiting for the time for bloodshed to begin, when he would steal through the churchyard, silent, covert, on his hunt for his prey. The Greenhouse watched through the nights but saw nothing. The man did not return. It was only the fox that slunk over the churchyard wall.

The Summer growth reached a crescendo before it faded into the first mists. The few leaves of the vines turned parchment yellow and fell singly to the floor, where they dried and browned and curled, to be swept away by the slightest draught, so light had they become. Vanessa grew heavier. The coarse black cotton of the dress she always wore tightened against her stomach until the gathers were all lost and the hem rose in front to reveal the top of the steel brace that was usually hidden by her skirts. She seemed tired. Her leg dragged across the floor in a way that it had not done before. Her daily life seemed so full of suppressed emotion that the Greenhouse was sure that she was sick. The shadow had entered her that terrible night, and since then she had always dressed in black, as if she was in mourning for her own self.

One early Winter day Vanessa started to tidy the Greenhouse as if time was running out. She washed and scrubbed the clay pots and the seed boxes, placed straw over the lilies to protect them from the frost, forked in some dried blood to feed the roots of the vines, and swept the floor of leaves, brushing them on to the steps, where they were caught up by the North-east wind and blown out across the lawns. There they joined with others to circle in drifts. Vanessa finally padlocked the doors and left. The Greenhouse ached for her as she walked heavily away towards the house.

The Winter was long and colourless. The garden yellowed under the frosts. Sapless trees blackened with cold. The leaden clouds in the sky pressed down upon the landscape, to be lifted only by the most vicious of arctic winds. The monotony of one sunless day upon another made the Greenhouse despair of ever seeing Vanessa again. She had locked herself away inside the house, as her mother had, and on the blackest afternoon when thoughts were bleak and came in brittle fragments, the Greenhouse closed its eyes with ferns of ice and waited for Spring.

It was a frosty morning. Pale sunlight teased the snowdrops and yellow Winter aconite to open their tight-closed petals. A large cock pheasant grubbed amongst the sodden mossy grass on the lawn; hunger led him to brave such exposure. The ash-coloured lichen that clawed tight on the walls of the house had been part prised from its host by the cold, and dripped dark smudges down the stone. There was a movement from behind the house: the farmer's wife attending to her livestock. Her cock crowed several times; he extended his neck feathers in a brief dispirited show to his hens, who wandered lamely away from him, scratching as they went, as yet unprepared to acknowledge the distinctive scent of the coming Spring.

The Greenhouse waited for Vanessa. Another day, another week, another month passed and there was still no sign of her. The windows on the front of the house were still permanently shuttered. The frost-locked soil softened, and through its wet mantle came bare-stemmed coltsfoot, but even with the change of season the Greenhouse still despaired.

The white magnolia opened its petals to the April light only to have its bloom destroyed by a spasm of frost so brutal and unexpected that Winter might have returned and, looking out at its leafless branches clinging to their stained limp petals, the Greenhouse could only lose hope, until suddenly, from on top of the wall a starling, beak gaping, wings spread, threw its throaty territorial squawks at the cold air in a defiant declaration that it was indeed Spring. Swallows arrived in search of the remnants of their ancestral clay nests. The woodpecker earnestly drummed in the trees. A solitary bee, glass-bound within the Greenhouse and tormented by light, struggled clumsily for its freedom until, exhausted, it fell and died as the sunlight it craved stroked its barred fur and polished its outspread wings.

There was a noise behind the house, a small cry attended by the soft burbling sound of Vanessa's voice. She appeared carrying a white wool-wrapped bundle in her arms. She spent some time wandering around the outside of the house, checking the Winter damage to the climbing roses, admiring their new red shoots, before coming to the Greenhouse. The image of Vanessa that had dimmed in its memory was as real and sharp and bright as the sun on its frost-cracked panes. Her return, as the sap was rising in the trees, the fierce acid-green leaves and swelling buds breaking through cold clay earth, taunted the Greenhouse like the wind that shifts from the North-east towards the West, carrying on its back the lament of Winter. The baby in her arms, so vulnerable, pale and white, was as intangible as the first snowflakes that fall and melt against the last heat of the year, until by their very mass they are able to cling together, hidden crystals of ice extending their complex structures towards one another, linking up to form the chilling chain that smothers everything from the light.

Vanessa turned on the hosepipe. Water began to flow freely, flooding the earth trenches of the vines. It combined with the dried blood, taking with it the residual smell down to the roots. The buds would soon burst into life on those vines that had been planted on the day that the child was conceived.

Vanessa returned to the house. The water flowed and bubbled throughout the afternoon. The miserable circumstances that had led to the existence of the infant seemed to have been completely erased from Vanessa's mind by his birth. She was slim again, the tired black dress was replaced by different clothes that fully exposed the leg iron. Her deformity was no longer hidden, as if for the first time in her life it did not matter. Her once untidy hair was now massed in shining waves. She was more handsome than the Greenhouse had ever seen her before.

As dusk came and the trenches were almost entirely filled with water the Greenhouse waited for Vanessa to come and turn off the tap. The water rose to the edge and swelled against its own surface tension until it burst and began to flow out across the tiled floor. It crept and ran down between crevices, as dark as the shadow of the man. The stain grew larger and larger until it seemed it would consume the entire Greenhouse. Terrified, the Greenhouse heard the vixen scream. The torn narcissus head rose and burned white in the sky. The fear of that long, shadowed night and the desert of the day that had followed spurted upwards, the life blood of a nightmare. The helpless white creature, the baby Edgar, was born out of a cursed night, the progeny of a demon. The infant carried the seed of his father who had now entered their midst in the guise of this innocent auburn-haired baby. Only the Greenhouse knew the dreadful secret of his source. It would never be able to forget. It would never be able to tell.

Through the dark came Vanessa alone; she turned off the tap and went back to the house. All night the Greenhouse felt a chill as the stain was sucked deep into its earth.

*

Every day Vanessa would come to the Greenhouse bringing the baby with her. She would lift him up in his basket on to one of the planks supported by chains from the roof that used to hold the epiphytic orchids. The Greenhouse thought that Edgar was very like one of those rare cosseted blooms, dependent for their existence upon the support of another. He was fed by his mother as those plants had been fed whilst clinging to their decayed stumps of wood. His skin was as translucent as their waxed petals and his eyes were flecked with patterns like those used by the orchids to attract insects.

He would lie for hours in his cradle, sleeping, then wake suddenly and cry. Vanessa would leave whatever she was doing and go over to rock him gently to and fro. He would stare emptily towards the sky, his eyes the colour of a clear day.

The feeling of loneliness and neglect that the Greenhouse had suffered through the winter lessened as the days lengthened and the frost came only at night. Vanessa divided her time and care equally between the Greenhouse and Edgar. The vines were given their first pruning. They formed small buds as the sap rose in their stems and they fed on the dried blood. Boxes of seeds were carefully planted, ranged in rows along the floor beneath newspaper and old broken panes of glass that had once belonged to the Greenhouse. The mercury in the thermometer that hung on the wall rose steadily as the month passed and the Greenhouse felt the quickened pulse of activity within it. Minute cotton furred roots travelled through catacombs made by the particles of soil. Pale bent shoots emerged, arching above the surface of the earth to uncurl their leaves. The Greenhouse fulfilled its purpose by capturing the warmth of the sunlight and keeping out the sharp wind whose edge could cut a seedling at a blow.

About the outside walls the nettles grew pale as the lime trees, until they were removed by Vanessa, later to be stifled by the succulent leaves of the belladonna lilies. Clove-scented wallflowers stood on top of the wall, brilliant blood reds and yellows. The dead matted tussocks of couch grass turned green. As May approached it seemed possible for the Greenhouse to look out and count to infinity, so great was the number of plants to be seen.

One day during that May at the war's end the church bells began to ring. Singly at first, then as each bell took on its own rhythm another joined. It was as if the entire planet was filled with sound. Elated and vibrating, the Green-house was unable to understand just what had caused this extraordinary disruption. The bells went on and on, swelling their combined volume in an ecstasy that the Greenhouse associated with the spiral of joy it had heard once years before, when the sound of music being played in the house had floated out of an open window, crossed the lawns and come in through its doors. The rooks in the elm tree rose in the air, but, instead of resettling, they coiled upwards in a cloud across the water meadows, followed closely by the wood pigeon. The peal ceased and gave way to a single summoning bell whose solemn call filled the Greenhouse with foreboding. Then the church organ's low tones drifted dimly from behind the house.

Vanessa came to the Greenhouse less during the following weeks. She seemed unusually preoccupied with the house. Shutters were unbolted and windows everywhere were thrown open to the air. Dust sheets were taken from the furniture and shaken out with carpets on the lawn. The front door now opened regularly and its hinges were oiled. Weeds were pulled from the gravel and roses tied back against the walls. The house was being prepared for Hugo's arrival home from the war.

On fine days Vanessa would cross the lawn carrying Edgar and place him on a rug at the foot of the steps to the Greenhouse. Then she would go back to the house to fetch a basket filled with a small picnic of bread and ham and cider from the farmer. She would eat, then lie with her head propped against the stone pillars at the top of the steps and close her eyes with the baby cradled in her arms until she was woken by his demands for food. During these times, feeling the soft pressure of Vanessa's body against it and the look of bliss on her previously troubled face, the Greenhouse felt entirely content. The shadow receded and it was overwhelmed with warmth.

Inside, the vines flowered and were fertilized by bees. Their fruits swelled into small conical bunches of grapes. The lilies emerged from their pots carrying long heavy buds that promised huge blooms of perfection. An unending scent of happiness seemed to stretch ahead.

One July day a silver car drove along the track to the house, turned on the stones and parked facing the Greenhouse. Inside was a man, a young woman beside him with short ash-blond hair. The couple sat talking to one another for some minutes until the front door opened and out came Vanessa, Edgar propped on her arm. The Greenhouse watched as the man it now recognized to be Hugo stepped out of the car and went to embrace his sister fondly. The young woman remained seated inside, eyes jealously watching the brother and sister reflected in the rear-view mirror. They separated and Hugo led Vanessa to meet his companion. She opened the door herself and got out and distanced herself from them by the car's long bonnet. She did not smile or move but stood in her high-heeled shoes, awkwardly balanced on the gravel. She wore a fashionable camel-coloured coat over an expensive cream silk summer dress. Her steely cap of hair tilted as she extended a gloved hand towards Vanessa. The warm smile on Vanessa's face vanished as Hugo introduced the stranger as his wife. Edgar squealed, distracting Vanessa, and before either of them had said one word she turned away from the woman, took hold of her brother's arm and led him away into the house.

Hugo's wife stood abandoned. She was unlike any woman that the Greenhouse had seen before. It was not only the expensive perfection of her clothes, the immaculate polish of her reddened nails, the sharpness of her that made her unfamiliar, but the fact that she was urban, an alien in the landscape. She glanced towards the Greenhouse, unappreciative of its magnificence and its purpose. She then surveyed the extent of the grounds before turning on her heels to look up at the house. She smiled to herself; she now knew that she was fortunate to have married Hugo. He was sickly after the injuries that he had sustained during the war. He would not live to a great age, and one day all this would be hers. She adjusted the handle of the shiny crocodile-skin handbag that hung over her forearm, tweaked at her hair and moistened her lips with her tongue, as if standing before an imaginary looking glass; then with newfound confidence she followed the others into the house.

Hugo emerged once again to collect two suitcases from the boot of his car; he carried them with some difficulty up the steps and into the house. The Greenhouse welcomed his return but it feared, even from its brief distant look at him, that he had been irrevocably altered by the war, by the new world that he now inhabited, and particularly by his wife.

There was no further sign of activity until dusk when all the lights were turned on inside the house, a sight that the Greenhouse had almost forgotten. It could heard the sound of voices. Edgar cried and then slept. There was a dull flicker of candlelight and the murmur of conversation from the dining room echoed across the damp grass, stirring memories of the past.

Out of the dark, like the two-dimensional inhabitants of

a once familiar painting, came Vanessa and Hugo's parents, friends, relations, servants and gardeners, gathered together on the lawns. Their presence shone in the dark with the strange aquatic light as when pools of sunlight penetrate through a dense canopy of green growth. Their numbers swelled and thinned as men and women drifted across the lawns. In the shade of trees and hedges, children, heads together, were party to a battle between two stag beetles.

Vanessa, in a long muslin dress, tripped on the skirt as she struggled to catch up with Hugo, who was crawling single-mindedly towards the stream. Pitying looks passed between the men and women as she tried to pick up her small brother and stumbled, tearing her frock on the leg iron. She gathered her skirts up about her waist, revealing to everybody the full extent of her deformity. Her father cried out to her in rage. Conversation faltered on the lips of the guests. They stood locked together, silent witnesses to a domestic calamity. Vanessa turned away red-faced, bursting with tears, her dress still held high, and lurched towards the Greenhouse. She had shamed her parents in front of all their friends. Hugo was caught by his negligent nurse and taken away. The conversation began again and the unhappy child sat on the Greenhouse floor, hands pressed tight against her ears, imagining the tones of pity and disgust in the murmuring voices outside.

There had been occasional approaches from the people of the village during the war. An old keeper had called each

Christmas Eve and left a brace of pheasant on the steps. More recently the rumour of Edgar's birth had brought two women to the house. With mixed feelings of curiosity and compassion they came to see the recluse and her infant for themselves. The Greenhouse watched as they waited on the front steps and pulled the handle of the bell. It tinkled inside but Vanessa did not open the door. One of the women was fat. The hem of her cotton dress wavered above her knees, pulled up unevenly by the rolls of flesh that hung about her hips. She wore a crocheted cardigan that was so tight across her breasts that the open-work holes stretched to reveal almost uninterrupted the huge sunflower pattern of the cloth beneath. Shapeless legs plunged straight into a pair of surprisingly small shoes that might have belonged to somebody else. The other woman was taller and, although she was well proportioned, looked scrawny beside her companion. She wore a dull brown felt hat at odds with the summer day.

They tried knocking at the door. The slimmer woman tilted her body backwards to look up at the windows. The other settled her feet, her weight rooting her to where she stood. Vanessa eventually appeared from behind the house, Edgar in her arms. The two women looked at one another. There had been gossip in the village but this was the first real evidence of the child's existence. They introduced themselves and exchanged some pleasantries. The fat woman opened her bag and produced a silver coin that she pressed into the infant's fist for good luck.

Edgar turned purple in the face and screamed convulsively as it touched his flesh. It spun out of his hand and up into the air like quicksilver. The three women looked down at the rejected gift which lay tarnished at their feet. Uncharitably, Vanessa turned her back on her visitors and the superstitious act that had so upset her baby and, without a word, went back to the house.

The two stood outraged at their treatment by this woman in the face of their kindness to her bastard child. They had come to bestow a symbol of their acceptance of Vanessa into their maternal community. They turned away and crossed the lawn towards the limes. As they walked their bodies twitched with self-righteous anger and excitement at being able to report to the entire village all that had taken place that afternoon.

The Greenhouse was uneasy about the return of Hugo with a wife. It had imagined that he would come to live with his sister; that all would be as it had been before the outbreak of war. Now uncertainty hovered like the black and yellow flies that flew indecisively, as though unable to make a choice between one flower and another. A misty slice of moon rose on its arc and faded at dawn.

Vanessa and Hugo were seated inside the Greenhouse, a hurt silence between them. They did not look at one another but stared straight ahead, out across the lawns. This was the first chance that the Greenhouse had had to take a closer look at Hugo. He had altered. He had aged. It showed as a weariness in his general countenance, a coarsening in his skin, lines about his eyes and a vertical furrow between his eyebrows. By contrast Vanessa's complexion had softened and her greying hair had become brighter. Delivered from the care of a baby brother and the burden of an invalid mother, she was delivered too from the sense of shame over her leg brace that separated her from others; she shone with a new vitality now, with Edgar to look after, and she felt liberated and no longer saw herself in the role of the helpless cripple.

Hugo had always been given all the attention. If great things had been expected from one of them, Hugo would have been the one to fulfil them, not the frail little girl with the twisted leg. Looking down, the Greenhouse felt some pride that Vanessa loved it, for it was certain that she was the more admirable of the two. Hugo had been robbed of his youth by the war, and for that the Greenhouse felt sad. But it could see that although those years had changed his outer appearance, he was still a weak, dependent adolescent.

Vanessa broke the silence, saying that she was sorry that she had not written to Hugo about the child, but that Hugo had not written to her of his marriage. Neither of them had been able to reveal the single most important shift in their affections. The Greenhouse felt secure, knowing that, now Edgar had been born, Vanessa would not leave it. But Hugo, the Greenhouse realized, was jealous: the role that he had always taken in his sister's life was being usurped by her son. Hugo himself, though, had chosen another woman; he had deserted his spinster sister. But the presence of the child surely released him from guilt. Vanessa was no longer solitary. She had Edgar and, whether Hugo liked it or not, she needed him less than he may have hoped.

Hugo showed some tentative curiosity about the father of the child. Vanessa acted as if the man had never existed, avoiding any reference to him. It could have been a virgin birth as far as she was concerned. Hugo ventured to ask if she had had an unhappy love affair. She ignored the question and the Greenhouse could see that Hugo was relieved. The child was enough, and the thought of another man was more than he wished to acknowledge.

Hugo turned to look at his sister; her profile was dark against the sunlit foliage, her arms bare, freckled with exposure to the light of an English garden. Her hair was caught up untidily, escaping wisps transparent against the light. Her face was free of make-up, its contours needing no further definition than her wide grey eyes. She was to the Greenhouse and, as it knew, also to Hugo the most beautiful woman in the world. Hugo stretched out his hand and touched her shoulder. She turned to him and smiled, happy that they were together again in the peace of their beautiful lost few acres. There should be nothing to mar the perfection of this reunion. Hugo got up and stood behind Vanessa's chair, placed his arms about her and leant forward to kiss the nape of her neck. She threw her head back against his chest and rested there for a while, feeling the close warmth of his body. Then she freed herself from her brother's embrace, got up and, taking his hand, led him close beside her out of the Greenhouse, down to the stream, past the globe kingcups and into the water meadows. The Greenhouse watched as they disappeared against the horizontal blue lines of the trees.

Hugo's wife was standing at the front door of the house while Edgar cried softly from within. She had been watching the brother and sister walk arm in arm, so obviously close to one another. The Greenhouse felt a small chill as she abruptly turned her back on them and re-entered the shadows.

Hugo's wife hardly left the house for the length of her stay. Not once did she come to the Greenhouse. While Vanessa and her brother explored their past together, she remained apart. Occasionally she would sit out on the lawn in a canvas chair, her platinum-dyed hair pulled back off her face into a headscarf that she wound into a turban. Her skin gleamed with the cream that she used to protect it. Her body was rigid in the open air beneath a sundress that was tied up in a tight bow at the back of her neck. Merely sitting outside required a great deal of preparation. Beside the chair, Hugo would place a table, magazines, her cigarette case, an ebony holder, a silver lighter, an ashtray, a cold drink, sunglasses and countless other whimsical articles that to her were essential charms against the evil eye of nature. She would lie absolutely still, like an Egyptian queen in her tomb surrounded by funerary objects. If an insect landed on an exposed part of her flesh, she would jump up, flapping her hands about her, and call helplessly for Hugo. Full of reassurances he would come to humour her, sit beside her, comfort her and attend to her every demand. Hugo was plainly besotted by his capricious new wife.

The Greenhouse watched. Hugo's wife realized that the brother and sister shared something from which she would always be excluded. She was jealous, and determined to separate her husband from the influence of his sister and his sentiment for the land. She abhorred the country. Everything about it depressed and frightened her: the extra hours there seemed in the day; the earthy smell of the insect-ravaged flowers; the constant noise of birdsong that woke her in the early morning and interrupted her bath before dinner; the interminable boredom and sameness of it all. Above all, she hated the colour green – it reminded her of the arsenic-coloured wallpaper that had hung on the musty walls of the depressing Victorian villas of her childhood.

The couple left. It was a premature departure, for Hugo had intended to spend the entire Summer with Vanessa but his wife's disconsolate manner shortened their time together and drove him away from what he had once loved and always would love more than anything else in the world.

Vanessa was sad to see her brother go. The Greenhouse, too, had become familiar with Hugo's presence, but their sense of loss retreated as Vanessa returned to the daily care of the plants and her child.

Months passed and the tiny fist that struck the air as the baby lay cradled in the Greenhouse became the infant that learned to walk, stretching his fingers out, grasping at anything that would help him to pull himself upright. The boy copied his mother, filling clay pots with earth and emptying them over the tiles, sprinkling the contents of his tiny watering can on to the vines, arranging seed boxes and cuttings into neat rows, piling raffia strand upon strand with the obsessional precision known only to the logic of a child. The Greenhouse was captivated by him as it watched each new discovery made, each new skill mastered.

Blissful years followed, punctuated by sporadic visits from Hugo and his wife. Vanessa seemed to have forgotten the man who fathered her child. Her devotion to her son was total. But, despite her new-found happiness, Vanessa had lost some of her former strength. She was frail in confrontation with Edgar and repeatedly gave in to his whims. Within the sanctuary of the house and the Greenhouse this relationship between mother and child developed unchecked, so Edgar grew wild, roaming un-challenged, careless of the feelings of others and the world beyond.

Hugo presented himself as nothing more than an indul-gent uncle, arriving with presents and limitless tolerance. His wife found the child messy and incomplete, a tiresome adjunct to their lives. She despised Hugo and Vanessa for the joy that they took in his first half-formed words, his occasional acts of affection – a kiss, a smile, a gift of one of his chosen objects. She hated the way that he brought Vanessa and Hugo closer together, to the point where they might almost believe Edgar was their own.

The Greenhouse watched as Edgar struggled through this tangle of affection, for it was in this hothouse that the child was raised and fed on the love of Vanessa. Just as the bindweed springs from the side of the plant it captures and finally strangles, leaving its once so intimate companion to wither in a heavy-laden embrace; just as the ground elder creeps from rank soil under tight-meshed yew until a skewer of light turns its leaves green and it becomes rampant, overwhelming all that lies in its path, so Edgar grew. He learned, like the bee that finds the trumpet of a flower too long for it to suck out any nectar, to gnaw away a small hole close to the heart of the flower, where he could drink freely. He mesmerized Vanessa with his careless innocence. To the Greenhouse he was the sparkling surface of a stone that remains unturned while the primitive louse hides in the dark beneath.

Until Edgar attended the local village school all his days were spent in or around the Greenhouse. It represented the entire world to him, as it did to his mother.

On his introduction to a broader world Edgar became uninterested in the Greenhouse and his mother's activities. He preferred to kick about the farmyard, terrorizing the hens and kittens, hiding from Vanessa in the dark corners of the sheds so that she would often have to spend an hour or so searching for him at bedtime, only to discover that her dishevelled son had torn his school uniform and covered himself with engine oil or mud. This seemed normal enough behaviour to the Greenhouse, for it remembered how Hugo at the same age had discovered the fascination of the yard. Hugo however had always been good-natured and obedient. Edgar was different. He resented even the slightest restriction that Vanessa put upon him and was strangely unresponsive to her gestures of affection unless

50

there was something he wanted that only she could provide. Then he would smile and shower flowers and false kisses on his mother, who, in her innocent belief in the innate goodness of her child, succumbed to his desires.

As he grew, Edgar began to show more guile in his manipulation of Vanessa. One afternoon during the Easter holiday Vanessa went out. She left Edgar in the care of the farmer's wife, who was unable to pay much attention to the boy because her sow was about to litter. He came to the Greenhouse nursing a small black and white kitten in his arms, stretched up and placed the animal in one of the empty wire baskets that hung from the roof. He watched as its terrified blue eyes peered out over the rim. Its tiny claws were scrabbling to get a foothold, its hind legs falling down, trapped between the open wires of its swinging cage. The kitten finally flung itself down towards the hard tiled floor and fled to one corner bristling and spitting as Edgar came to catch it. He put out his hand and grabbed the frightened creature. It clung to him and sank its sharp little teeth into his flesh. He squealed and dropped the animal; it ran towards the vines and hid. Edgar was consumed with rage at what had happened to him. He watched as beads of blood swelled out of his hand. The Greenhouse let out a filter of hot air through its open ventilators.

Edgar, a fiendish look on his face, pulled out a thick strand of raffia that hung in a coil above where he sat. He knotted a loop at one end and passed the other through it to form a noose. The kitten froze where it hid. Edgar started to make squeaky enticing noises at the animal. A flurry of fur and the kitten was recaptured. Edgar pulled the noose over its hind legs and tightened it below its rib cage. It flew about on the end of the thin yellow cord and Edgar smiled at his victory over his helpless victim. The more it churned and twisted, leaping in the air, the tighter the cord cut, parting the shiny black fur to reveal a sharp gash of pink skin.

The Greenhouse, horrified by Edgar's treatment of the innocent kitten, longed for Vanessa to return. Outside the leaves flicked and turned in the wind and it began to rain. Edgar tied his captive up to one of the chains that supported a hanging platform. The kitten clutched at the air, howling with pain and terror. Edgar left and returned to the yard.

The kitten tired. The raffia cut harder against its flesh. Its struggle seemed to be over. Its starved body dangled, its lips curled back to reveal the fine white milk teeth. Its eyes closed. Its fight had gone. The Spring storm broke and raindrops fell through a gap in the Greenhouse glass, soaking the kitten. They ran down its upturned body and dripped from its pink nostrils on to the floor. The small puddle made a dark stain.

Vanessa returned, and unable to find her son came to the Greenhouse where she was confronted by the half-dead, sodden animal. She cut it down. It opened its eyes and stared at her blankly, all fear and strength extinguished. She stroked the back of its neck, feeling the twin sharp bones that stuck out at the head of its protruding spine, examining the scarred hindquarters. It squirmed and sneezed a fine spray of blood over her; it was crushed internally. It let out the tiniest little mew. Then a low sound came from its throat. Vanessa continued to stroke it as it purred itself to death.

For some time Vanessa was quite unable to do anything with the dead kitten. She clasped it to herself as if the warmth of her body would give it life; she prayed that it would show some sign that it was not really dead, for the knowledge that this was Edgar's doing was too much for her to contemplate. Vanessa buried the kitten at the far end of one of the earth trenches so that it would not be dug up by the fox. The wet pool on the floor dried, leaving a thin, pale film on the tiles.

Vanessa did not confront Edgar with what he had done. The child was too young to have understood the implications of his actions. The image of the wet cat dangling from a noose inside her Greenhouse haunted her. She buried it in her unconscious as deep as it would go. To have chastised her son would only have raised to the surface her worst fear – that the child was heir to the man, and that however much love she gave him she would be unable to influence the part of him that was entirely bad. Whenever she saw her son after that day, a black worm of memory would squirm inside her brain and she would fleetingly see the kitten sneeze away its life blood in front of her eyes.

Edgar appeared to have forgotten the kitten. He did not return to look for it.

The pig had a litter of ten. She rolled over in the night

and crushed half of them with the immense weight of her flesh.

Folly, a puppy of Meg, the black and white sheepdog from the farm, became attached to Edgar. He did not like her opaque blue, blind eye or the sheep ticks that clung about her throat and gorged on her blood, making nasty bumps under her fur. But he did enjoy the way that she obeyed his commands. She would crouch, ears cocked and nose twitching, concentrating on the boy's every move.

As the vines matured and began to develop edible clusters of fruit, Vanessa devised a ritual, a celebration to be shared by herself, the Greenhouse and Edgar alone. The fact that the vines had not been tainted on the day they were planted but instead had grown healthy and strong fed her hope that under her care Edgar too could be bred to perfection. The harvest of the grapes would be a way of bringing them all closer, a celebration of nature which had brought her such contentment and even given her a healthy son. It would, she hoped, be an occasion that Edgar would not be able to forget for his entire life.

When the bloom on the grapes matched the colour of the early Autumn mist that drifted between the woods and the water meadows, the time for the harvest arrived. Vanessa approached from the house carrying a basket, Edgar beside her. They entered and closed the doors against the chill of the late afternoon. Covering a small iron table with a white cloth, Vanessa placed on it a candle, some bread and some wine. Edgar sat down and watched solemnly as his mother took out a curved, razor-sharp pruning knife from her pocket. Gently and methodically she cut the tight bunches of ripe grapes and placed them in the wide basket. When she had harvested the entire crop she sat down and lit the candle.

The mist rolled in from the stream and spread in the twilight, covering the lawns like an incoming tide until it reached the higher ground on which the Greenhouse stood, now illuminated from within by the golden light of the candle's flame. The Greenhouse was like a great cathedral at Evensong or a tropical glasshouse marooned on an island in a limpid sea.

Vanessa poured a glass of wine for herself and one for Edgar. Together they raised their glasses and toasted the Greenhouse. It shuddered as the murmuring of their voices died high up amongst its glass, echoing the thin brittle sounds of the oncoming Winter.

When they had finished, Vanessa extinguished the candle, picked up the basket, took Edgar's hand and locked the doors of the Greenhouse before they made their way back to the house.

Melancholy hung within the Greenhouse as it watched Vanessa with her uneven limp wade through the mist that was so pale against the falling dark. Separation from Vanessa always saddened the Greenhouse. Through the worst of the Winter nights it was haunted by the memory of the kitten swinging from its braid, by the bark of the dog fox and the vixen's screams at night.

*

As he grew, Edgar came markedly to resemble the man who was his father, in particular his eyes and his tangle of reddish hair. He fostered a growing resentment towards the Greenhouse. It showed itself in small incidents when Vanessa's back was turned, or she was absorbed with tending the plants or the vines. He would steal into a corner and watch her sullenly until, unable to endure her lack of attention any longer, he would indulge in some small cruelty; a stick waved, breaking a pane of glass, a knife scored hard along the Greenhouse's ribs, a small plant uprooted from its pot and left unnoticed to perish from drought – insignificant acts in themselves but deliberately executed to cause distress either to his mother or the Greenhouse.

Even Folly the puppy suffered torment. One hot day in the Summer she climbed on to the edge of the water tank and leant forward to drink. Edgar pushed her in. So confined, she was hardly able to swim. He made no attempt to rescue her, to hold her collar or call for help to Vanessa, who was inside the Greenhouse. He just watched blankly as the pathetic creature splashed and swallowed the water, the weight of her sodden coat pulling her down further into the tank. The pale-blue blind eye bulged white round the rim with fear. It was only when Vanessa heard the splashing that she ran out to rescue the near-drowned dog. Folly was immediately sick with the water that she had gulped and lay shivering with fear on the grass. Edgar watched as his mother reassured the animal, then turned away and began to wail. Vanessa assumed that he was distressed by what he had just witnessed, but there was slaughter in his blood. Now that it had all gone wrong he was jealous of the attention that his mother paid to the animal; he screamed that she should come to him.

Evil had been implanted in Edgar by the man. This grew as he grew. It became more cunningly disguised as he became older but it was undeniably present, and the Greenhouse, after witnessing the cruelty to Folly and the kitten, was not able to trust the boy again. It felt only an increasing fear for Vanessa that in her maternal simplicity she would always refuse to acknowledge the truth. One day the man's shadow would consume Edgar and a devil would be let loose. But during the Winter the Greenhouse was always inhabited by memories and premonitions. The bleakness of its interior and the rime upon the land encouraged introspection that was as barren as the landscape.

After her experience in the water tank Folly deserted Edgar. Occasionally the Greenhouse caught sight of her amongst the hens under the elm but she came no closer. It missed her. Edgar himself only came to the Greenhouse for the harvest ritual. He had turned back to the farmyard for his amusements.

Hugo continued to visit each Summer but his wife would rarely be with him. His main preoccupation was with Edgar. As yet he had no child of his own, and he seemed increasingly to regard Edgar as his own son. This was for the duration of his stays. At other times Edgar received little attention from his uncle, who only remembered him at Christmas or on his birthday. Hugo, unable to resolve the conflict between his wife and his sister, compromised by separating the two. He might have neglected Vanessa entirely had it not been for his desire to have Edgar for himself.

It was after one of Hugo's visits on Edgar's ninth birthday that the Greenhouse saw the boy playing on the new bicycle that his uncle had bought for him. He was pedalling at top speed around the outside of the house and through the yard, scattering the hens and carving ridges into the gravel. Stones sprayed against walls and windows, frightening Folly away; tail between her legs, she ran into the dark recess of one of the barns and hid. The rooks raised their coarse cries of alarm and the commotion brought Vanessa out of the house. She called to Edgar to come for it was time for the harvest ritual. Edgar ignored his mother, turned his bicycle abruptly away and began to pedal in tight circles around the trunk of the elm. He hit one of its roots, lost control and fell. The bicycle lay beside him, its twisted front wheel revolving unevenly. Edgar got up, saw what had happened, and began to cry. Vanessa went to comfort him but in his fury he struck his mother repeatedly and ran away from her into the yard.

Some time later the Greenhouse watched Vanessa and the reluctant boy come towards it. Edgar was pushing the damaged new bicycle which moved erratically across the grass. He propped it against the Greenhouse steps so that he could see it all the time he was inside.

Edgar watched his mother cut the grapes. They sat in silence, tasting them and sipping the wine from the previous year's harvest. Vanessa shifted herself to face the boy and announced to him and the Greenhouse that she had employed a gardener.

The Greenhouse cooled at the idea. A stranger in its territory, a man with power. The idea of any change in the order of life was disturbing, so fixed was the pattern. A gardener would alter the landscape. The Greenhouse had experienced the presence of many in its past: men who cultivated order. They had laboured under Vanessa's father's obsessive instructions with the exotic and mysterious foreign flowers and fruits that he had cultivated, but they had not really cared for those hothouse aliens. The Greenhouse had often heard the men brought from the fields to work muttering to one another that it was an obscenity that a man should spend more on coke in one season to force an orchid to bloom than they would earn in a lifetime.

Edgar plucked a black grape from the bunch in front of him and threw it to the floor. His eyes were fixed upon his mother. They were black and wild, and so large that they seemed to fill his face. The Greenhouse and Vanessa looked into their frightening void. The candle flickered in a draught. The light inside the Greenhouse dimmed, then the flame swelled and steadied. Edgar's face was visible again, his skin sallow in the candlelight. Gone was the rose-coloured innocence of the small child. He was the image of his unknown father.

Vanessa gasped, turning her head abruptly away from the sight but he was reflected, as if in a looking-glass, in every single pane of the Greenhouse. Vanessa got up, her leg iron hit the metal of the table – a dull resonant noise. She nervously gathered up the cloth and bundled it on top of the basket of grapes. The boy sat still until she was about to blow out the candle, then got up from the chair. As he did so he deliberately placed the heel of his shoe on the discarded grape. He crushed it beneath his foot until the skin split and the juice flowed.

It was then that her night of horror came back to Vanessa. The black worm eased its path to the front of her brain. The dead cat swung to and fro as she looked down on the perfect child who had taken away her solitude. He grinned, the wide mocking grin of a demon with lips pulled back and gums gleaming with saliva. Momentarily her love ebbed away. She struck him for the first time in her life. Blood spat behind her eyes and slowly dried into tiny, hard, dark specks; they merged with a sudden burst of tears and softened into a mist of forgiveness.

Mr Thorne, the gardener, did not begin his work until the New Year. The Greenhouse watched uneasily as Vanessa spent the afternoon showing the man the grounds and giving him instructions. She did not bring him to the Greenhouse and to its relief it realized that its fears had been unnecessary. Vanessa intended to continue taking full care of the Greenhouse herself.

It was the end of the afternoon, when she had returned to the house, before the Greenhouse was really able to look at the man. He was down by the stream with a wheelbarrow and the young sheepdog beside him; Folly had apparently decided that this man was to be the new focus of her attention. He was working, thinning and splitting some of the irises and reeds that had spread and were choking the water. He laboured steadily on towards dark on that cold grey afternoon, hacking at the swollen roots, piling them into the barrow. From time to time he would stop to straighten himself and drop his head to look down into the water, like an ancient grey heron stooped over its prey. He seemed a melancholy, silent, gentle man who already merged with his surroundings. His presence caused no discord. The light faded and the gardener wheeled the barrow up from the stream. He crossed the lawns and passed by the Greenhouse, raising his cap to it as he went by. He might have done this countless times before, so little did he intrude upon the landscape. The last sight that the Greenhouse had of the new gardener that day was as he rode his bicycle along the track between the leafless limes, towards the wood and the village. Folly stood looking wistfully after him.

Edgar was not so easily satisfied. At the start he constantly harassed the man while he worked, subjecting him to a mixture of childish taunts and inquisition. Thorne did not ignore the boy entirely but his taciturn nature and solid lack of response eventually defeated Edgar. He lost all interest in the man.

Under Thorne's quiet care the garden grew. Blood-red climbing roses flourished, their flower heads expanding to the size of cabbages. Scented annuals filled the beds amid foxgloves, hollyhocks and delphiniums, whose spikes grew to the height of a man. Daisies and blue speedwell were almost eliminated from the lawns which, during Summer, were hatched with silver and green from Thorne's meticulous mowing. Beneath the boundary wall he planted sweet rocket and clematis that petalled the stone from Spring until Autumn. Aside from the garden Thorne's main preoccupation seemed to be with his patch of vegetables. They grew on the land that lay behind the Greenhouse wall. This the Greenhouse could not see. It would gaze jealously as each morning Thorne carried a trug of freshly picked vegetables to the house for Vanessa. But the Greenhouse had the vines. No harvest of tomatoes or beans, of lettuces or carrots could ever rival the grapes and it was only inside its glass enclosure that they would grow.

The vines constantly captured Vanessa's attention. Whether this was solely because of the care that they demanded or because of her need to be within the confines of the Greenhouse was a mystery. Even Edgar now took second place to her obsession. She no longer deserted the Greenhouse during the Winter but would spend hours behind its frosted glass, scraping away at the fibrous bark that formed along the stems of the vines so that they might not harbour the smallest red spider through the Summer to come. She scratched away until their stems were as smooth as those of a young tree, pruned and trained them to follow exactly the vertical ribs of the Greenhouse frame. Dusty white limewash ringed their bases to prevent any insect attempting to climb up and destroy their perfect fruit. She was waging war against an unknown foe who haunted unseen.

Vanessa never overcame her horror as she listened to the

farmer's pig scream in terror as it was released from its sty, chased into the yard and cornered before its throat was slit. Then the unforgettable smell of its hair being singed from its skin drifted from behind the house, followed by the sound of the meat cleaver hacking into its upturned carcass. She would sit in the Greenhouse with its doors and ventilators tight shut, hands pressed against her ears until it was all over. But despite her distaste, she would readily go to the farmer to collect the bucket of madder-red blood, and water it into the roots of the vines.

As Edgar grew Vanessa made every effort to ensure that his childhood was as normal as possible. She tried to rely on her brother to replace his unknown father. Many children had lost the men in their families during the war and it was not unusual for Edgar to be brought up by his mother alone. Hugo's attentions were inadequate and so she would pretend to her son that his uncle wrote regularly to ask about him. She bought presents in Hugo's name and insisted that he come to stay for at least part of every Summer.

Edgar was a lonely boy. He would rarely bring a friend home from school for tea or to play with at weekends, however much Vanessa encouraged him. He seemed to prefer his own company and as he grew older deliberately set himself apart from the village children. This disturbed Vanessa, and in an attempt to release Edgar from his solitude she invited the son of a distant relation to come to stay for a holiday.

From the time that Luke arrived, collected by the farmer from the station, to the time that he left, his face swollen with tears, Edgar made his stay unendurable. The soft, amiable child was taunted and teased and finally tortured until Vanessa was forced to send him home, unhappily altered by his few weeks with her son.

All had seemed well enough for the first few days and the Greenhouse watched as Edgar appeared to play with his new-found friend. Edgar showed the boy everything that interested him within the confines of the grounds. His current preoccupation was with collecting butterflies and moths. Together the boys gathered young laurel leaves which, when mashed, gave off volatile fumes from the small quantities of prussic acid that they contained. Edgar carefully filled the bottom of a jam-jar with the deadly pulp, covered it with a circle of blotting paper and pressed a thick cork into the jar's mouth.

They spent hours in the water meadows, Edgar lying on the grass, propped up on one elbow with his killing bottle held tightly between his knees, the collecting box at his side, while Luke tore about at his instruction, flapping a net in the air, tripping on molehills and tussocks of grass, relentlessly determined to please with the capture of a specimen. A success: a fine clouded yellow, its four saffron wings edged with black. The wings closed. It was drab except for its red legs and the brilliant gleam reflecting from its compound eyes. Luke hesitated as he was about to release the exquisite creature so that he might see its beauty once again, when Edgar called out to him, and the prize was carefully delivered for extermination.

Luke sat down beside Edgar and watched with awe as the killing bottle that he had helped to prepare was uncorked. Edgar raised it and thrust it under Luke's nose; the noxious smell of bitter almonds filled his lungs. Dizzy with fear and fascination he looked on as it was carefully introduced into the net. The helpless insect fluttered in, to be stupefied and asphyxiated in the volatile oil under the sealing palm of Edgar's hand. Luke blinked rapidly, his long eyelashes brushing his cheeks. He held his breath. The butterfly was dead. Edgar shook it gently from the jar, took a golden pin from the back of the lapel of his blazer, pierced it through the thorax and fixed it to the lining of the collecting box. Luke closed his eyes.

Bored with a surfeit of meadow browns, brimstones and fritillaries, Edgar moved on to the edge of the wood. Luke got unsteadily to his feet and followed. The Greenhouse watched the two boys kick and beat the trees to gather moths which Edgar imprisoned live in matchboxes to await a later collective death.

Dusk came and the boys returned excitedly to the house with their finds. Vanessa came out to the Greenhouse. She was relaxed, content, her confidence restored now that her son had at last found a friend. She trailed her fingertips across the coarse leaves of the vines, checked the lilies in their pots and breathed in their scent, before winding down the ventilators and closing the doors. She left the Greenhouse to the soft and sleepy night that consoled the landscape after the frenzy of the summer day.

*

Some hours after dark the Greenhouse was surprised by the rough sliding sound of a window being opened high up on the first floor of the house. It watched as Edgar lit a lantern and climbed out. He dropped down on to a narrow crumbling parapet of stone about a foot below the base of the window, setting the light down where it cast its rays wide into the dark. Then he eased himself along until he came to the next window, which was already open, and slid back inside, closing and fastening it after him.

Next came Luke, carrying the butterfly net. He perched beside the lamp and waited for the first nocturnal moths to be attracted to the glare. Several small dull ones fluttered towards the light; one stuck to the hot glass, charred and fell away into the dark below. Luke looked round for Edgar, and as he turned a huge death's-head hawk moth landed on the wall beside him. Quivering with fright at the size of the insect he dropped the net, which billowed in the air and wavered to the ground. Undisturbed, the moth rested while Luke tentatively put out his hand; it spread its banded wings as if to take flight. Luke trembled, his fear of the drop beneath him forgotten in the confrontation. He grabbed it. It squeaked like a bat, wriggled and scrabbled its legs against his skin, but Luke held on. He was filled with pride that he would be able to deliver to Edgar the greatest prize of the night.

He started to ease himself along the parapet to what should have been the open window. He found it closed. The Greenhouse heard a lump of stone fall on to the gravel some twenty feet below where Luke was clinging with one hand to the thin wooden astragals that divided the glass. He edged his way back to where he had climbed out. Just as he was within reach of safety, Edgar leant out, laughed fiendishly at the frightened child and pulled the sash tight shut. The boy called out to him. The lamp burned into the night. He was too high up to jump. His hold on the frame was insecure. He screamed and howled but he was not heard; his cry could have been that of an owl or a fox in the night. He screamed again, sobbing with terror. Vanessa was woken and looked out. Luke cried to her. The Greenhouse saw lights appear inside the house as Vanessa went to rescue the boy. Luke stood rigid, the moth boxed in his closed, sweating fist. He unclenched it to show her, revealing fingers dusted with microscopic scales from the creature's wings. Its thorax was crushed and a sticky liquid oozed from its abdomen. The wings themselves were stripped of their beautiful dust, reduced to transparent, veined membranes. Exhausted, damaged and flightless as the moth, the boy stood abject before Vanessa. She closed the window and bolted all the shutters from within. The lamp continued to burn all night. In the morning a score of insects lay dead on the ground.

For the next week the boys spent their time fishing for trout in the stream and building camps in the water meadows. One evening before sunset Vanessa closed the Greenhouse after turning on the hosepipe to flood the vines so that the grapes would continue to swell; the water would encourage the roots to feed on the dried blood.

The two boys had been making a fire down in the meadows. Dissatisfied with their attempts to cook the small fish that they had caught, they left its charred remains and crossed over the bridge to the Greenhouse.

Edgar began to collect some leaves that had piled up against the wall and had not been cleared by Thorne. He carried them to the East windows of the Greenhouse and put a match to them. There was a sudden blaze as the sun-dried leaves caught for a second, smouldered and went out. Edgar looked at Luke. The Greenhouse recognized that look. It had seen it before whenever Edgar was about to commit some dreadful act. Luke was frightened and started to run away towards the house, but Edgar caught up with him and pulled him back. The boy bent to Edgar's will. He went about collecting anything he could lay his hands on that would burn. Edgar waited, clutching the box of matches, as Luke heaped dry grass and twigs against the Greenhouse frame. Edgar drove Luke on while he himself hid out of sight of the house until he was satisfied with the size of the potential bonfire. Then he struck a second match. The dry grass lit; it crackled and flamed. Luke, driven, as if he had lost all reason, continued to bring fuel to the fire, too terrified to stop. He knew nothing of the Greenhouse except that it was Vanessa's. He had never been inside it during all the time he had stayed. He felt the danger in Edgar's controlled excitement at the sight of the enormous blaze that flared up. But so dominated was he by Edgar that he did not have the courage to stop him.

Unlike the fire that they had built so unsuccessfully in

the meadow, this one burned. Orange flames shone through the glass, disguised by the brilliant reflection of the setting sun. The Greenhouse knew that Vanessa would be unable to see from the house what was happening. The heat intensified as its own wood caught fire, charring as the flames swept up its dry surface. After the initial searing the flames licked and sucked at the open wounds, taking a firm hold on the Greenhouse. Edgar watched as his dutiful friend worked furiously for him, carrying more and more fuel to feed his fire. Vanessa came to the front door to call the boys in. The sun had set. The flames behind the Greenhouse tore into the dusk. She ran, crying with confusion when she saw what was happening. She caught Luke in the middle of the lawn returning with a pile of twigs in his arms. White-faced, he looked up at her and dropped the wood. It scattered at his feet. Vanessa ran on, leaving the boy slumped in a nest of despair. Edgar, seeing his mother approach, slunk away and hid in the churchyard.

Vanessa opened the doors of the Greenhouse. She brought out the hosepipe that had been watering the vines and put it into the heart of the flames. They hissed and lowered, flickered and steamed, until they were quenched. She pulled the debris away from the Greenhouse and turned off the tap, checking the vines and locking the doors before she left. Luke was still rooted to the place where he had dropped the twigs in the middle of the lawn, sobbing helplessly. Vanessa went to comfort him and guided him back to the house. There was no sign of Edgar. The Greenhouse watched out for him where he hid. The moon rose and at last he emerged from the shadows. After sliding over the churchyard wall he crossed the grass to the house. When he reached the gravel he stopped at the sounds of his footsteps and approached cautiously peering in through each window in turn, before slinking round the side to the back where he was lost from sight. Next, from inside came the noise of angry voices. The lights turned on in the rooms upstairs and their shutters were locked.

The next day Luke left as he had arrived, with the farmer. He was quite broken. Vanessa hugged him warmly on the steps of the house but he did not smile as she waved him goodbye. Sadly Vanessa came to the Greenhouse. Her leg iron weighed heavily on her for the first time in years. She looked at the dark stain, the charred scar burnt into its frame. Vanessa sat inside the Greenhouse and wept.

It was Edgar's eleventh birthday. The Greenhouse had watched the boy spend the morning down in the water meadows, lying flat on his stomach behind a hummock of grass and firing his catapult at a family of moorhens on the banks of the stream. Because he had to hide from his mother as well as his prey, he was too far from the water birds to do more than alarm the hen. She removed her brood upstream and hid among the reeds. Edgar, bored by his lack of success, cast about for another target. He saw the glass of the Greenhouse flash in the light. He crossed the bridge and walked a few yards along the bank. The Greenhouse shuddered as it realized what the boy intended to do.

He reached into the pocket of his shorts for one of the pebbles, lodged it in the leather of the catapult between his thumb and forefinger and raised the forked stick to the level of his eyes. Slowly he drew back his right arm as he pulled the elastic taut. He squinted, took aim, then loosed the stone. It curved in an arc, fell short and was lost in the long grass. The Greenhouse trembled with relief. The boy searched his pockets for another pebble. He kissed it before placing it in the catapult. He raised his arm and took aim. The Greenhouse saw his face contort. The pebble left the catapult at such speed that it flew straight to the Greenhouse, breaking a pane of glass. Fragments fell and splintered across the tiles. The Greenhouse rang with pain. Edgar laughed and reached into his pocket. The Greenhouse braced itself. Intent on destruction Edgar failed to hear a car approaching along the track. He loosed a third stone, which struck one of the wooden ribs, sliding down the glass into the gutter. At that moment Hugo came shouting across the lawn and grabbed him. Vanessa ran from the house and stopped still as she saw her brother beat the protesting boy, who pulled away and ran, red-faced with rage, towards his mother. She cried out weakly after him as he passed her and fled into the churchyard.

Hugo's wife got out of the car and walked towards Vanessa, smiling. With a haughty jerk of her head, she raised one eyebrow and looked inquiringly at her sister-in-law. The scene she had just witnessed pleased her. It confirmed what she felt about Edgar; that he had grown wild and was quite out of control. The boy was too old to spend his life locked away with an unmarried cripple for a mother. A boarding school would discipline him. The smug triumph on Hugo's wife's face so irked Vanessa that she turned away and went to join Hugo inside the Greenhouse. She looked up at the gaping hole in it, took a brush and started to clear away the glass. Hugo looked at his sister. He thought that she should have attended to the boy before the Greenhouse. He drew up two chairs, asked her to sit down. He was grave. Vanessa knew what he was about to say: that Edgar was of an age to be sent away to school. She listened staring at the broken glass at her feet, as Hugo went through his carefully constructed appeal. He was sure she would agree that it was for the boy's welfare. Vanessa felt forced to comply. She said nothing, only stared out across the grass to where Hugo's wife still leant against the car smoking a cigarette. The Greenhouse noticed that huge tears rested on Vanessa's cheeks. She leant forward and they fell to the floor leaving dark splashes on the dusty surface of the tiles. Her hand stretched out to pick up a fragment of glass and she raised it up in front of her eyes. She studied the rainbow of light reflected along its splintered edge, then dropped it. It made a barely audible noise as it shattered.

Edgar went away the following September. For the first time since she had planted the vines Vanessa was alone for the harvest. That Autumn was exceptionally mild. Mist hung over the meadows all through the day. On the chosen afternoon Vanessa arranged the Greenhouse as she had in the past. A clouded sun hung low in the sky behind the cedar. Damp was already rolling up from the stream. It brought with it a thick silence that clung like moss to all it enveloped. The Greenhouse was soon covered by this airless white shroud. A soft melancholy hung over everything. Vanessa could not escape from it.

She cut the bunches of grapes and tasted them. There was no lifting acidity, nothing to stir her from the emptiness that she felt but she stayed on until it was dark. The mist outside turned to a fog that thickened and pressed against the frame of the Greenhouse. Like vaporizing dry ice it crept through cracks and under doors. A bleak soulless Winter stretched before them.

Thorne carried on with his solemn labours through the first frosts. The vegetables grew thin and it was with some pleasure that the Greenhouse watched a monotonous supply of leeks and cabbages being carried to the house.

Winter gripped. The Greenhouse spent most of its time with frosted panes. Vanessa obsessively tended the vines, removing the fruit-bearing lateral shoots and scraping away at the ragged bark until all that remained of each plant was its bare spine, its entire life-force reduced to a single stem. Vanessa grew thin, her appearance dishevelled, her spirits as heavy as the iron on her leg. Time dragged. She had lost all will to lighten the load and the world beyond had ceased to exist for her. The Greenhouse watched her flounder. Half-light overwhelmed the greater part of the day, drowned even the rising of the sun under the clouded surface of its sullen grey lake. Vanessa sank deeper into her despair. The cold gnawed away at her fingers and ran down her back. It cut hard into her thoughts. Ice chilled her soul until all that she felt was a North wind whose bleak breath penetrated every second of the day and the night. It pinioned the song of the birds before it left their throats, taking away with it even the echo of joy.

Vanessa would spend entire nights inside the Greenhouse. She was watchful again, waiting for the return of the man. The Greenhouse too started to look for him, often sure that it had seen his shadow disappear over the churchyard wall. But no-one came. Edgar did not return during his holidays. He would stay with Hugo, and did not come to see his mother. The Greenhouse wondered whether Vanessa watched through the nights for the man or for his son.

As the years passed she lost hope for Edgar. Her time for nurturing and feeding was over. She knew that like herself, Hugo would fail to change Edgar, that he too would concede to her son. Edgar was stronger than either of them. The Greenhouse witnessed Vanessa's increasing torment as day after day and now year after year she lived alone with it, tending the vines.

Summers ceased to bloom. It rained, and the gravel around the house filled with puddles that did not seep away even on the occasional hot June afternoon. House martins gathered together like shoals of black and white tropical fish, collecting mud for their nests. It rained, and the puddles merged into lakes of silted water. The roots of the grass in the lawns were saturated and they did not grow. Instead, mosses that had always hidden just below the surface erupted into raised mats that burst millions of spores amongst the blades around them. It was so wet that Thorne was unable to mow, and so they spread their falsehood of bright green unchecked. Flowers swelled their buds against their own verdant growth only to be spoiled in a night of icy rain. Roses hung limp and broken from their stems, stained from dark red to brown. Yellow pollen ran in rivers along the petals of the flowers and dribbled to the ground before it could be gathered by the bees, who were felled by a single raindrop. Damp permeated everything and the landscape turned such a sickly shade of green that the Greenhouse almost longed for Winter.

Thorne still carried his vegetables to the house but they had split and burst as they gorged on the water. Their tops were pale from lack of sunlight, bloated and slimy with decay.

It rained ceaselessly in Summer, snowed in the Winter, and hailed in the Spring. The grapes on the vines were few and would hardly ripen before the air bred the grey mould that ultimately destroyed the fruit from within. Vanessa tended the Greenhouse and the vines, and each Summer she waited for Edgar.

Hugo would write endless apologies. She knew that they were lies and sometimes she would cry inside the Greenhouse, but the sound of her tears was obliterated by the noise of the rain washing down the gutters and flowing through the pipes into the water tank outside. There was no-one to hear her save the Greenhouse. It longed to relieve her of her emptiness but it could not. So her misery continued until one day when the Greenhouse saw her

75

almost run from the house across the lawns towards it with a letter in her hand. She flung wide its doors, opened its ventilators in spite of the wind and the rain and called out aloud with happiness that Edgar was coming back. The Greenhouse felt the humidity within it evaporate, and shuddered as the cold rush of air froze the moist condensation that clung to its glass.

It was Edgar's sixteenth year. It was a harsh Summer's day. There had been no rain since he arrived and the air was gritty with drought. Edgar had been home for a month, and during that time had found a girl from the village. He brought her to the Greenhouse. She stood before it, awed by the extraordinary grandeur of the old hothouse. Edgar pushed her forward but she hesitated to enter, for she had heard stories of the Greenhouse and of how Edgar's mother devoted her life to it. Some said that Vanessa no longer inhabited the house; that she lived in the Greenhouse, that Edgar must be the result of some monstrous union between Vanessa and an unnatural plant she cultivated under the glass. Vanessa had never been seen to associate with a man, except her brother. It was in this myth that the gossips hid their fear that Edgar was the result of incest. The children of the village believed the story. The girl's round face flushed at the thought of it as Edgar took her hand and led her inside, closing the doors behind them.

Under the glass the temperature was equatorial, the humidity saturating; combined with the filtered green light this gave the girl the sensation of being under water. The mature vines with their lush foliage stretched to the full height of the Greenhouse. It was how the girl imagined a tropical rain forest to be as she looked up at the canopy of green that hung overhead. She was afraid that some outsize insect lay hidden between the leaves and would fall. She shuddered, certain that she could see the plants growing, even hear them. She tried to remove her hand from Edgar's grasp but he held her tight. Her skin went white under the pressure of his grip. With frightened eyes she looked at him, her fair curls flattened and her summer dress sodden from the wet air under the glass, waiting for him to take her out of the Greenhouse. She tried again to pull away. Water saturated her lungs, she was unable to cry out. Edgar bent forward to kiss her, and as his face came closer it was not tender but brutal and frightening. His strange pale skin and auburn hair were foreign to her. She was accustomed to the florid English complexions of the boys she had grown up with. But she succumbed to his kiss. It had been so much what she had wanted to happen. The Greenhouse looked down at the silly, even stupid, young face and saw that this innocent was there to be used by Edgar to hurt the woman that he most despised.

Edgar let go of the girl and crossed the Greenhouse to the table, where he had noticed there was a pair of shears. He picked them up and started to cut at the stems of the lilies that stood upright in their pots. He moved quickly along the rows. The coarse edges of the blades squeezed and tore at the tough stems of the flowers. They leant and fell to the floor, bruising their waxy petals and showering them with pollen. The Greenhouse was powerless to stop the boy. The temperature rose by degrees. Edgar gathered the flowers from the floor and piled them into the arms of the girl. She was overwhelmed, naively believing that this was a sign of true love. To her this was what happened to film stars and princesses.

They left the Greenhouse with its doors flung wide, and headed towards the stream, the girl still clutching the lilies. The Greenhouse looked down at the massacre that had taken place. Outside Edgar and the girl cooled their feet in the stream and laughed away the remainder of the afternoon.

Vanessa was shocked by what she found when she came to the Greenhouse. She paced up and down hardly able to look at the uneven stumps that jutted from the pots. All the Greenhouse's finest lilies gone. She took a knife from her pocket and started to prune each empty stem with a smooth diagonal cut. With care they would grow again. Vanessa forgave Edgar for what he had done, allowing that this was his first love and had rites associated with it. At the end of the Summer he would return to school and the girl would be forgotten.

The Greenhouse was filled with an unformed dread, and as August came and the trees turned from their early Summer paleness to a leaded blue it knew that Edgar's malice towards it had not declined. Huge, threatening cumulus clouds rose heavy in the cobalt sky, promising but never bringing rain. Cracks appeared in the close-mown lawns. The stream slackened. On sultry nights the dense clouds became so oppressive that it seemed they would crush the Greenhouse under their weight.

The storm did not break. Vanessa sat in the Greenhouse, dispirited. There was no change. Just the glittering harshness of the sun at its zenith and the brooding afternoons. The grapes swelled and hung in their sooted bloom high upon the vines. Even Thorne seemed parched by the heat and spent much of his time in the shade of the house, distractedly weeding the gravel. Edgar and the girl spent every day together, though they did not come to the Greenhouse.

During one of those sultry August nights when the sky was electric with storms Edgar was inside the Greenhouse and as each flash lit his face with its unreal light the Greenhouse saw that there were tears in his eyes. A stifled sob murmured inside him, a cry like that which comes from the throat of a small child left alone in the dark, clinging to his sadness for comfort, in the hope that the balm of his misery might lull him to sleep. There was a terrible hush broken violently by an explosion of green light that spilt across the sky, startling Edgar out of his thoughts. He began to finger the clay pots, gently toppling them one by one off the staging in a wanton, childish way. They rolled over the edge and smashed on the floor. The Greenhouse was gripped by terror: Edgar, as if possessed by the charge in the lightning, spread his fingers wide and ran towards the vines. Clasping his hands around their thick stems he twisted them from where they grew. Their sap rose as he wrenched them from their ties; they creaked as they were forced away from the Greenhouse and hung, limp and broken, towards the floor. Grapes fell and were trampled by Edgar in his orgy of destruction. He stopped and breathed heavily from the effort. The black sweating figure finally clenched his fist, thrust it through a pane of glass and fled out into the fiery night.

It was that last act that woke Vanessa when through her open bedroom window came the sound of breaking glass. The Greenhouse saw her look out, but all was still. She retreated into her bedroom and the Greenhouse was left quite alone.

Sap bled from the vines. Bruised air floated about in the Greenhouse. It watched the last flash of light as the storm ended. Edgar had vanished.

The sky cleared, the moon rose high and its ashen light entered the Greenhouse. Broken fragments of pots, like headstones in a graveyard, cast jagged shadows on the earth-strewn floor. A slow-worm squirmed, coiling its head into its tail. A throbbing pain sucked at the roots of the vines and the Greenhouse longed for Vanessa, but she did not come.

It was early the following morning before the Greenhouse saw Vanessa. She was standing under the elm tree at the back of the house talking to Thorne, who had just delivered his vegetables. The Greenhouse watched as she lifted a huge globe artichoke from the trug that Thorne held out for her and threw it into the air, catching it before it fell by its massive, leaved stem. She looked in the direction of the Greenhouse, noticing its open doors and the broken pane of glass; she remembered the sound that had woken her in the night. She let the outsize vegetable drop and started to move as swiftly as she was able towards the Greenhouse.

Once inside she spun around as she tried to take in just what had happened. Her entire body sagged as she slid down on her heels, her back against one of the iron columns. She fell sideways on to her iron-cased leg and with tear-filled eyes started to pick distractedly through the debris. A frail heap on the Greenhouse floor, she sobbed huge gasping sobs as the awful truth invaded her: it could only have been Edgar's work.

Vanessa stayed on in the Greenhouse, trying to retrieve what she could. The temperature rose as the day progressed. Huge sulphurous storm clouds gathered outside. In the afternoon Edgar with the girl crossed the water meadows, on their way to the stream. Vanessa closed the Greenhouse doors against the approach of her son, watching the two of them as they settled on the bank between the reeds. They started to kiss. Vanessa and the Greenhouse were transfixed by Edgar's apparent tenderness towards the girl. It seemed impossible after what he had done the night before. Vanessa continued to work, tying the vines back to their supports, binding their stems where the milky sap still flowed so that they should not bleed to death. She re-formed the barrier between herself and the sight of the two young people on the river bank. The twisted leaves of the vines hung limp, their blue undersides facing the light.

Vanessa noticed a sudden frenzy of activity from the bank. Edgar was on top of the girl, who appeared to be struggling against his attentions. The Greenhouse and

Vanessa caught their breath and watched as Edgar tore at the girl's summer dress. She continued to struggle. Edgar struck her roughly. Then he pulled up her skirt, covering her face in a cloud of cotton and forced himself between her thighs. Vanessa was paralysed with horror as she realized that her son was raping the girl.

As if it were made of glass, her heart broke. A fragment of pain seared her. Its force travelled to the tips of her fingers. Her body shuddered. Blood-red colours filled her eyes as, blinded by sunlight through her closed lids, she slid unconscious to the floor. The Greenhouse looked down at her where she lay surrounded by smashed terracotta. Blood flowed from a gash in her side.

Edgar rolled over on his back, sated by orgasm. The girl in her shock and innocence rearranged her clothing as if this propriety could erase the event. She stood up and looked at Edgar, who lay remote from her, his hair sweatily matted with grass, his mouth composed in a slight smile; a malicious smile, which she assumed was mocking her for the indecency of the act she had submitted to. She pulled at her hair as if to tidy it. Edgar did not stir. Then she wailed out loud as she ran away towards the lime trees and village. The story was true. He was the child of a monstrous union. An unnatural man. Edgar fell asleep where he lay.

The inside of the Greenhouse was in turmoil. It strained with every rib of wood and every rod of iron to make Vanessa get up. It felt warm blood draining from her limp body, seeping across its tiles where they sloped to the earth at the foot of the vines. Her blood joined the absorbent particles of soil; they filled slowly like a sea sponge with the remains of her life.

Edgar got up, brushed himself down and walked idly away in the direction of the trees. The sky was thick with massing clouds. Steely rays of sunlight cut through them to the ground making a rapid shifting pattern on the landscape. The Greenhouse was helpless with relief that Edgar had not come to see how it was that his mother lay dead; that Vanessa was to be left entirely to its care; that they should be alone at the end.

There was an enormous clap of thunder. A boiling torrent of rain fell from the skies. Lightning, white fire, fled among the clouds. Water flowed over the Greenhouse with fury. Only this explosion, this anarchy of the elements, could equal the rage it felt. The Greenhouse stood battered as water streamed, wave upon wave, over its glass.

Vanessa's body lay still in the gloom. The outside air cooled and misted the Greenhouse panes. Tiny drops of water formed together into transparent beads; they slid silently down the glass, joining with others to make larger drops. The leaves of the vines dripped. The storm passed and in its wake came silence, so that all that could be heard faintly from within the Greenhouse was the terrible sound of grief.

Edgar did not return to the house that afternoon. There was no sign of anyone. The Summer storm had done little more than temporarily fill the cracks in the earth before the water was evaporated by the blistering sun. Plumes of steam rose from the long grass, forming a haze over the water meadows. Time passed so slowly that the Greenhouse imagined it was to witness the decomposition of Vanessa's corpse. A brown moth landed on her outstretched arm, opening and closing its wings several times to the sun before fluttering away to the underside of a leaf. Still no-one came. The Greenhouse expected to see Thorne, but he appeared to have retreated even from the shade.

In the distance the Greenhouse could hear the mechanical noise of a harvester at work, and watched as the field turned from ripe gold to be furrowed with stubble.

The vines now shaded Vanessa's body with dappled light. A lock of hair covered part of her face. She lay like a robin with a thorn in its breast where the blood had flowed, soaking into the cotton of her dress and merging its red rose pattern with the white background before spilling to the floor to feed the vines.

Through the night the Greenhouse kept vigil over its lost love. Dawn came, drying its tears into streaks on the glass. Cold blue early light filled its interior. The body of Vanessa lay contained in its sepulchre. The glass palace built to celebrate life was now ash-pale, its plants bled white, its ribs bleached like whalebones, its earth parched. It clung to its wall; its soul had fled.

The sun rose. Through the East windows of the Greenhouse a patch of light inched across the floor; like an incoming tide it swept towards the body, lapped at the tips of Vanessa's fingers, touched her hair and kissed her eyelids before flooding over her. A sharp-edged battle was fought between light and shade. The Greenhouse longed to be able to close its thousand eyes but its curse was that they should be for ever wide open. It was forced to look, though it shrank from the sight. No longer hidden by the comforting twilight, the hard cold fact of Vanessa's wretched stiffened corpse lay in its midst. Under the blaze the Greenhouse ceased its mourning, stirred from its sadness by the first unfamiliar feelings of hate.

It was midday. The sun was so high that it cast no shadow. The house stood empty in the vertical light. White-faced stone stared out on to colourless lawns. Windows hung on their cords, empty, half-raised between the dark and the light. The front door lay open. The slate-tiled roof divided the sky. The house was still. A spider scuttled loose-legged across a ceiling and down one of the walls to hide in a corner. Outside, nothing moved. Only the surface of the water in the meadow glittered as it flowed downstream. The Greenhouse stared out into a landscape that was awash with light.

Edgar approached along the lime avenue and went inside the empty house. It was late afternoon before he came out and crossed the lawn. He stopped at the rising ground in front of the Greenhouse, just as the man had done on the day that Vanessa had first been stained with blood. He looked up at the huge glazed structure, its roof arching away from him. The Greenhouse looked down on Edgar and saw him as a malevolent animal, a beast of rapine, who had preyed on the frailties of everyone he had known. His auburn hair shone with a false fire made by the sun. His face was obscured but its outline was unmistakable. He was the reincarnation of the man whose seed had taken form in Vanessa's womb.

`Unlike the man he did not hesitate, but started to climb the bank until he stood on the steps and cast his own shadow through the glass. The Greenhouse braced its structure. The boy entered, crushing fragments of clay pots beneath his shoes. He stopped when he saw his mother, crouched on his heels to take a closer look, ran his hand over the patch of dried blood, savouring the smell. He pushed her hair back from where it lay limp across her face, his fingers leaving two brick-coloured smears across her cheek. He moved his hand down to feel the rigid flesh of her neck and shoulder, then smiled down at the bruised creature that lay at his feet. He left the body of his mother on the floor. The Greenhouse resolved upon revenge.

The farmer set light to his field of stubble. Through the open doors of the Greenhouse came the smell of blackening straw. A breeze blew from the South bringing with it cindered clouds of smoke, choking the air with fumes. The fire was so bright that it rivalled the sun. Fast-moving flames swallowed and cremated everything in their path. The landscape was scourged by countless dragons, spitting red venom. Sparks rose beneath the shadows of their scaly black wings and spread ominously towards the wood. The sun was eclipsed by the surge of swelling smoke and with it all sight of the church tower, the cedar and the house vanished. The Greenhouse and the body of Vanessa were smothered in the scent of hell.

The fire burned out. The air cleared to reveal that the edge of the wood had been singed. An open black scar festered with smoke behind the lime trees.

Edgar returned with Thorne, who was carrying a stretcher made of two metal poles with a steel mesh between them. He placed it alongside the body, then he stood back and removed his cap. His usually passive face twisted into a hopeless look of anguish as he took in what lay before him: Vanessa's body in the devastated Greenhouse. Thorne shook as he wrung his cap between his callused fingers and muttered an inaudible prayer. He leant down and gently blew from her hair the cindered straw that had drifted into the Greenhouse. It rose on the soft current of his breath and resettled within her shadow. He got up and searched for a broom to sweep away the smuts that surrounded her. Sooted dust clogged the turgid air. Thorne swept harder and harder, scraping the stiff bristles across the tiles, leaving ash-coloured scores on their surface. Dust of earth, dust of blood and dust of fire filled the Greenhouse. It pierced the air with its stench. Particles clustered together and grew to the size of grit that stung against flesh and glass alike. Edgar recoiled at the sight of Thorne's eyes: the whites were veined with tears of exertion as, with one final effort, he pushed at a pile of broken terracotta. It tumbled in a ruddy waterfall down the steps, falling heavily to lie in an eddy of sharp curves on the blades of the long grass below.

Thorne looked up at Edgar. The boy turned away from

the gardener and paced to the furthest end of the Green-house. The dust began to settle, clasping itself to itself, layer upon layer like the close-meshed scales on a moth's wing. Edgar snatched at a bunch of unripened grapes from one of the vines, and squeezed until the juice flowed out between his whitened knuckles and trickled on to the tiles. Thorne watched. Edgar stared out of the Greenhouse towards the village. Thorne waited. Edgar began to laugh. At first it came as a trickle. Then he threw back his rufous head and the laughter flowed. His whole body began to twitch and the laughter poured. He turned upon Thorne and his laughter gushed out; like the black tongue of a viper it searched and swept through the Greenhouse. In the midst of this animal hysteria Thorne leant down to manoeuvre Vanessa's body on to the stretcher. Clasped in her fist was a torn vine leaf. Edgar's jaws locked in silence. Thorne arranged Vanessa's bloodstained dress and closed her eyes. He glanced about the Greenhouse and taking a pair of secateurs from his pocket, cut a single scented white lily which had opened its petals that day. He laid it on her breast then stood up breathing heavily, confused, murmur-ing to himself in the silence. Edgar came forward; the two men raised the laden stretcher between them and carried it down the steps, through the long grass, across the lawn and away into the house.

Within an hour the doctor had arrived. The Greenhouse watched as all the shutters were closed upon the fine Summer's day.

*

With the night came dark warm Summer rain so fine and soft that it seemed to comfort all that it covered, finally quenching the last smouldering ashes in the field. Inside, the Greenhouse still felt the body of Vanessa lying there in a shapeless mass on its floor. It remembered its past of oranges ripening among their dark shiny leaves, pineapple raised like some primitive offering above their fleshy spikes. As the clouds cleared the moon sat reddened and low in the sky. The time for slaughter arrived and the fox, the owl, the weasel, took over the night. The Greenhouse filled with unformed fears for its fate that were aggravated by the smallest movement of an insect or the shrill cry of a hunting animal.

The dark patch of blood still stained the floor, its shape changing and blurring as the moon traced across the sky. It lay there like an inescapable black thought, representing a future just as unresolved as its shape. Nothing could take it away.

Later that night Hugo arrived with his wife. They went swiftly into the house. After a short time Hugo came out, went to his car and switched its headlamps on full. The sickly yellow light shone across the grass straight to the Greenhouse, forming two paths between which Hugo walked towards the glittering panes. He entered, saw the chaos inside and paced from one end of the Greenhouse to the other in the strange slanted light, until he noticed the patch on the floor and knelt down to examine it more closely. With the realization that this must be his sister's blood, he got up and searched for a watering can which he filled from the tank. Standing above the black eye of the stain he tilted the can over it, as if watering a rose. The water puddled and its dusty surface began to drain towards the vines. Hugo went back to the tank, refilled the can and repeated the watering. This he did five or six times until the mark had gone and the floor of the Greenhouse had been washed clean.

Hugo sat down with his head in his hands. Straining his fingers against his scalp, pulling at his hair between clenched knuckles, he began to cry. Uncontrollable sobs shook him. The noise of his misery writhed and twisted itself out of him into the air and was echoed by the Greenhouse. They were joined together in a lament for the loss of the only human being that they had both loved.

Hugo fell silent and stood up, his swollen face streaked with tears. He looked at the mutilation of the vines and the bandages that stemmed their bleeding sap, at the pots of lilies without their flower heads; slowly he came to understand what had happened. It could only have been Edgar who had caused this destruction. He had watched the boy grow up into a creature who had lost all control over the savage side of himself. He saw that this brutish, wanton behaviour had been designed to torment his mother in the way that would hurt her most. Edgar had tried to destroy all that remained for her to love and Vanessa had died of a broken heart. Hugo cried out again in a rage of despair, for he knew that he too shared the guilt for her death. He had taken her child away from her. Vanessa had died alone.

The fox stirred from his earth, roused by a scent on the

wind. He crossed the lawn and his eyes, their vertically elliptic pupils narrowed, glowed green in the light from the headlamps. Hugo left the Greenhouse and, as he walked back to the house, a musky smell hung in the air.

The church bell began to toll for Vanessa's burial. The Greenhouse watched as the coffin was carried from the house, followed by Edgar, Hugo, his wife and Thorne. The farmer, the farmer's wife and a few others were already inside the church.

The Greenhouse listened to the tones of the organ. There was a long silence before it caught sight of the gathering as it left the church and proceeded past the low wall to the grave where Vanessa was to be buried.

The small group returned to the house for a time before parting. Hugo stood beside Thorne on the front steps. The two men were unfamiliarly dressed in dark suits. Formality clung to Hugo; he was sombre and full of remorse. For the first time in his life he took responsibility for the house and the land. He brought Thorne to the Greenhouse, instructed him as to how he would like it to be looked after in his absence. There was to be a new coat of paint and any rotting ribs were to be replaced. The glass was to be cleaned of all the green algae that clung to it, the vines tended, loose stones repaired and tiles relaid. Only plants that had been grown by Vanessa were to be cultivated. Nothing was to change. Hugo saw the Greenhouse as a permanent memorial to his sister. No-one was to enter. Edgar in particular, whatever excuse he made, however much he threatened, was never to be allowed inside the Greenhouse again. A padlock was to be fitted to the doors and only Thorne and Hugo would have the keys. Thorne listened quietly, comforted by what he heard.

Hugo took the opportunity to question Thorne about the events that had taken place during that Summer. Hugo was certain that the gardener knew more than he had told, but the man was not forthcoming, and without his co-operation there was little Hugo could do. It was unfair to press him. Vanessa had just been buried and the man's sorrow was plain. He should be left to grieve. Hugo made some practical arrangements with Thorne about money and assured him that he would never have to worry about his employment so long as Hugo lived. Thorne nodded. The understanding between the two men was confirmed.

In his new-found strength Hugo decided to confront Edgar and question him about the devastation of the Greenhouse, to try to find out what had actually happened before Vanessa's death. He looked down at the floor and saw the stain of his sister's blood where it still clogged the fissures between the tiles. Resolve grew out of his anger and his grief. The youth was sly and cunning, he knew, but Hugo intended to bring him to account for his actions.

Edgar stood almost as tall as Hugo and looked directly into his uncle's face. He had shown no shock or sadness either before or after the burial of his mother. Nor had he been seen to associate with the girl from the village since the day he had raped her. He was sullen. He did not understand what it was that Hugo wanted of him or why he had been brought to the Greenhouse for this confrontation. He was irritated by Hugo's endless questions. Edgar's futile attempt to claim his mother's attention by his attack upon the vines had failed. His cry for her love, to which he felt entitled and that he had lost, had failed. Vanessa was dead. All that remained was the Greenhouse. He despised Hugo for trying to make him share his grief.

The boy turned away and pulled at one of the unripe bunches of grapes. On tasting one, he screwed up his face at its bitterness and threw the rest on to the floor, kicking them into the trench. This act enraged Hugo, so frustrated was he by his interrogation and inability to extract any remorse from the boy. To be dismissed by Edgar with this wanton gesture made him shake with rage. His belief that the death of his sister had in some way been precipitated by Edgar made him react in a way that was alien to him. Impotently, Hugo struck out and battered the boy with blow after blow to his head. When he stopped, his fists and palms were bruised. He looked down at his fingers trembling limply. Edgar's cheeks were flushed. There was a small cut on his inner lip and a trickle of blood oozed from the inside of his mouth. The boy did not move; one eye began to swell. Hugo stepped forward to catch the boy's sleeve, as if to seek pardon for what he had done. Edgar turned viciously like a predator, and spat in Hugo's face. Pink foam of blood and sputum sprayed over Hugo's cheek. Edgar shook his arm from Hugo's grasp and left.

Hugo restrained the urge to go after him. He stood weak and confused about just what it was that he had really intended to confront Edgar with. He despised himself for his action. His hand throbbed. The violation of Vanessa's sanctuary was all that he had actually witnessed of Edgar's malice. His sister was dead. For that they were equally to blame. Hugo left, locking the doors behind him.

The Greenhouse was abandoned, its tenuous love for Hugo evaporated. For Edgar its feelings grew as coarse as the stem of a mature bramble, as sharp as a weasel's teeth sinking into the neck of a rabbit. They spawned upon themselves like botrytis amid vegetation on a damp Autumn night. It was Edgar, who had destroyed Vanessa. Only the Greenhouse understood, but it was powerless to communicate even a scrap of its anguish as it watched Hugo, ridiculed by Edgar, follow him back into the house.

Several days later, before leaving and locking up, Hugo came to the Greenhouse to see how Thorne had managed. The vines were bandaged and tied back. The tiled floor was spotless. The pots of lilies were ranged neatly along the inside wall. The pane of glass had been repaired. Thorne was the most capable and caring of men. As Hugo turned the car in front of the house the Greenhouse saw Edgar looking out of the rear window. It knew that he would return to complete his destruction. The car drove away, leaving a trail of dust between the avenue of limes.

As the time for the harvest of the grapes arrived and they swelled to perfection the Greenhouse became sad, realizing that the harvest ritual would no longer take place. Thorne came to cut the fruit, but he did it in his methodical way, taking the best of the bunches and packing them carefully into boxes to sell in the village. One day he sat down to roll himself a cigarette but he did not taste the grapes.

Folly, the sheepdog, had become his sole companion. She went everywhere with him, but she would not enter the Greenhouse, however hostile the weather outside. She would sit on the steps and peer through its open doors, ears cocked, waiting for Thorne.

A year passed and there was no sign of Hugo or Edgar. The Winter had almost robbed the Greenhouse of any ability to feel pain. The black wet days went on long into the Spring, turning its existence into a dull ache as it looked at the house with its shutters drawn and doors bolted. Thorne continued to grow his vegetables, but these too went to the village. The Greenhouse felt as if the land were being managed by an absentee landlord, and that was very much the case. Thorne cared, there was no doubt of it now that he was master of the garden, but there was no-one to appreciate his work except the Greenhouse. All it could do was endure the flood of memories as the lilies once again began to stick their fat shoots from their pots. Finally the Summer came. The vines spread their leaves across the Greenhouse glass, the first lily burst its swollen bud and curved back its perfect petals. The Greenhouse's longing for Vanessa erupted with the formation of that first flower. It thought of Edgar, of how he had deceived and despised his mother, of all the futile love that Vanessa had given him. It thought of how that love had masked from her the truth that the black seed grew within him. Only the Greenhouse could put a stop to his rampant evil before the bud burst and spread its rottenness on to the earth. The Greenhouse withdrew from the dreadful thoughts that gathered as lily after lily bloomed and lavished its scent over its companion.

A car arrived, Hugo's car. As always it parked facing the Greenhouse, and out climbed Hugo, his wife and, to the Greenhouse's terror, Edgar. Thorne greeted them and they turned away to go into the house. As he had done on leaving, Edgar stopped to look at the Greenhouse. It trembled, and a loose pane of glass slipped a fraction, leaving a gap through which escaped one of the vine leaves that had been pressed up against it. The Greenhouse knew what it would have to do. In all its years spent clinging to the wall it had never had to make an independent decision of such gravity. When the right moment arrived it would seize its opportunity; meanwhile it waited.

Hugo came to inspect the Greenhouse. When he unlocked its doors he was intoxicated by the contained scent of the lilies that flooded out like a tidal wave. Inside the heavily shaded glasshouse, light passed through the lush growth of leaves, falling in points on the floor like a warm Milky Way. The humid air clung to Hugo's skin. He was enchanted. He imagined Vanessa to be sitting inside as she so often had; he could even smell the sweet earthiness of her skin. Her presence lived on here in the Greenhouse like a heart pulsing in its enormous frame. The place was not, as he had feared it might be, a dead shrine to her misery; it still glowed with her warmth.

He sat there until it was dark, talking quietly but audibly, confiding his regret to his sister. He told her that if he had had a choice he would have come to live here with her, sadly recounted how he no longer loved the young woman that he had first brought to the house, and how he had discovered that she had never loved him. More, that she had always been jealous of Vanessa. For that, the blame was his, because he had always loved his sister more than any other woman in the world. He had wanted Edgar because he was part of Vanessa, but he had lost him. While Edgar had been at university after Vanessa's death, they had become virtual strangers.

His self-pity was anguished, and the Greenhouse wanted to reach out to him. He got up, embarrassed by his outpouring, and put his hands deep into his pockets so that he might stop himself touching anything inside the Greenhouse, as if even the slightest caress of his fingertips would soil the memory of his sister. He submerged himself in the scent of the lilies and the vines, felt the misery of all those lonely years to which he had condemned his sister. He saw everything with the harsh clarity of retrospective understanding, which does not allow one single act to be redeemed. Hugo felt more helpless than he had ever been in his life. He looked up, noticed the slipped pane of glass, then left.

Edgar did not approach the Greenhouse at all. Each

morning he would set out from the house in the direction of the village and not return until after dark. He behaved like a man who was trying to make as little contact with his surroundings as he could. Twice he looked as if he was considering coming to the Greenhouse but then decided against it and went off in his usual direction. He seemed to have changed little. The auburn hair was still thick in clouds about his pale face. The large features had thinned but his ravenous eyes were as they had always been. It was the sight of those eyes that maintained the Greenhouse in its resolve. All it had to do was wait, and waiting was the greater part of its life. It had stood for a long time and would stand for as long as it took.

Autumn came early, and the leaves of the vines had just begun to turn yellow. The grapes hung heavily on their stems waiting for Thorne to cut them and take them away. He had looked after them well, and with maturity the crop had increased to a substantial size. The Greenhouse felt a mellow satisfaction as it watched the last martins and swallows wheeling in the skies in their restless preparation for the sun. They left, and the Michaelmas daisies flowered, bending their white and lilac heads towards the earth under the increasingly heavy dew. Thorne picked the last of his tender vegetables and stored away the apples before the first frosts. Dead leaves gathered against the wall of the Greenhouse. The wet south-westerly wind that had been blowing for several days started to shift towards the East just before dusk, cooling the vaporous air and everything to which it clung. There was a faint rustle of sodden leaves. Condensation began to form on the panes of the Greenhouse as the temperature fell outside.

A figure approached from the woods across the water meadows. The Greenhouse strained through its clouded panes to see that it was Edgar. He was carrying an axe over his shoulder, a bundle in his other hand. On crossing the stream he did not follow his usual course towards the house but turned to walk unsteadily over the lawn to the Greenhouse. His boots left tracks in the dew-laden grass. A gust of wind twisted through the fretwork along the Greenhouse roof. Outside, the exotic rosy blooms of the belladonna lilies gaped open, wide and defenceless against the night frost to come. The Greenhouse froze as it saw that Hugo had not padlocked its doors. Edgar came inside.

He untied the bundle and took out a candle; he struck a match and ran the flame over the candle's base before lighting the candle and sticking it to the table. Beside it he placed a near-empty bottle of the wine that Vanessa had made each year from the grapes, and a piece of bread. Edgar was there for the harvest ritual. The axe stood with its cold blade resting against one of the iron columns. Edgar began to cut the bunches of grapes, one from each vine. The Greenhouse was filled with the warm glow from the candle. Its feelings about Edgar mellowed: he had returned to celebrate, as he had as a child with Vanessa. He was still part of her. It watched as he took a swig from the bottle of wine and realized that the boy was drunk. Edgar smiled to himself, beamed broadly and then began to chuckle. The charge of excitement in his laugh travelled up to the ribs and glass in fragmented shock waves and was lost to the night. The Greenhouse no longer rejoiced that Edgar had returned and remembered the harvest. Its last hope perished on the change in the wind outside.

Edgar continued to eat the grapes and drink the wine until he had finished the bottle. It was dark outside and the house was shuttered. Smoke from one of the chimneys was blown across the lawn and seeped into the Greenhouse, bringing with it the smell of charred wood. It remembered the fire lit by Edgar and his cousin, the attempt to burn it to the ground. The dog fox barked from the other side of the churchyard wall. Startled by the noise, Edgar struggled to his feet and went over to pick up the axe. He swayed sideways, knocking it to the floor. The candle still burned.

Drops of wax fell on to the floor. Edgar bent down to pick up the axe, looking furtively about him; only his eyes moved. The axe blade gleamed silver in the candle light. The wind dropped to a faint roar in the distant wood. The cedar's branches rippled in a slight swell. Edgar was tense. Slowly his fingers curled around the handle of the axe. The boy rose. His shadow was thrown by the candle light across the floor and at right angles up the limewash wall. It was immense, twice the height of Edgar, stretching almost to the top of the Greenhouse. He raised the axe slowly above his head. The shadow on the wall grew as the arc formed by his arms came together where his hands gripped the shaft of the instrument of death.

As his body paused before he brought the full force

of the blow down on the thick stems of the vines, the Greenhouse saw his head thrown back and his face illuminated from below by the single candle. It was the face of a grotesque beast, a chimera, its features swollen into one another. In that instant the Greenhouse let loose the slipped pane of glass. It fell from above him and severed the neck of the monster. The axe sprang from his clasped hands, spinning and turning with a life of its own, flashing in the light before it struck the ground, and on to its blade fell the full weight of Edgar's body, sprawling upon the tiles. He shuddered. For a moment his fingers clawed at the earth at the foot of the vines. His blood flowed in a torrent, spread like a lake across the earth to be sucked up by their roots. The candle guttered as the wick burned away until, with a watery spit, it went out. The Greenhouse was filled with the strong waxy smell of its blaze and stood bolted to the wall, shaking in the windy night.

It was Hugo who discovered Edgar's body. He saw the axe, the fallen pane of glass, the remains of the harvest ritual. He looked about him, numbed by what he saw. He was silent. He showed no horror; he was almost relieved that it was all over. There was nothing that he could feel for Edgar. As for the fallen pane of glass, he had already noticed how it had slipped and not been repaired. He had not mentioned it to Thorne. An accident, a macabre coincidence, he need not pursue it further. All that was required was to call the doctor, have the body removed and repair the pane of glass.

The procedure was straightforward. Edgar was buried beside his mother. There were few mourners, and Thorne did not attend. When the group returned to the house after the burial the Greenhouse was surprised to see the girl with whom Edgar had spent a summer, the girl he had forcibly taken on the bank of the stream. She was dressed entirely in mourning. The Greenhouse saw again the golden curls framing her sad face beneath her small black hat. After looking in the direction of the Greenhouse for a while, instead of following the others indoors, she turned away. Her tiny solemn figure started to walk steadily towards the village. The Greenhouse watched as Hugo ran after her. He caught up with her under the lime trees and they exchanged some words. She shook her head and continued on her way. Hugo did not persist but walked slowly back to the house.

That day by the river altered the course of the girl's life. She could not forget that Edgar had taken her against her will on that stormy, sulphurous afternoon. The memory of her adolescent longing for the pale-skinned, evil boy, of her drowning in the scent of the pillaged lilies that he had piled upon her, of her intoxication in the face of the decadent, unfamiliar smell of lust and revenge, had remained with her. She had walked four miles across rough land to attend Edgar's burial, wanting to know something more of the young man she believed had loved her. But, standing with Hugo and the other mourners, she found herself even more removed from Edgar than she had been since their separation. Now, as she continued on her way and entered the wood, she began to thread the spindle of

102

her memory as if she were still Edgar's princess, locked forever in the turret of a faery castle. Slowly she turned the spindle inside her head and wove a cloth of perfect fiction, threading half-truths and lies through the conscious and unconscious recesses of her brain until a web had formed within her of such complexity that in her entire lifetime she would never unravel a single truth. She was cursed by the belief that, had Edgar lived, he would have come for her. She was certain that the faithless boy had loved her. It was the only way that she could lessen her deep shame at her lost virginity.

Thorne continued to look after the Greenhouse and the garden. The solitary man moved silently, never missing a day. His devotion was complete. Hugo came every Summer to stay for a few weeks. He still hoped that he could return to live in the house but his wife prevented it. The time that she did spend there still filled her with misery even though Vanessa was dead. She only looked happy on days when she could go out with the car to the nearest town. Hugo tried to make the Summers more amusing for her by inviting her friends to stay; he would organize outings and picnics, but she never overcame her intense dislike and fear of the country. She did not visit the Greenhouse and found it sinister that Hugo would sit inside it for hours. She would stand at the border of the lawn and call him to come out.

He would pretend that he had not heard her, but, however great her frustration, she would never cross the long grass to fetch him. She was afraid of the Greenhouse and did not understand what power it had over the strange unhappy family into which she had married. Hugo's sentimental attachment to it now that his sister was dead did not allow her jealousy of Vanessa to wane. If he died before her, as he certainly must since his injuries were steadily undermining his health, she would sell the house, the Greenhouse and the land without hesitation. Meanwhile her dislike festered impotently.

During the long months when the house was empty Thorne and Folly did what they could, but they were both growing old and it was impossible for them to keep the garden as it had been. At first, small things were neglected. The once-perfect lawns now harboured dandelions and daisies. The long grass that had previously been mown after the narcissi had died was now left until midsummer for its first cut. The yellow flags in the stream seemed to carry an ever-increasing number of flowers. Along the Greenhouse wall brambles and bindweed scrambled through the flowers. But Thorne did not neglect the interior of the Greenhouse. That was kept as it had always been when Vanessa was alive.

Hugo was frail and prematurely old. His body became thin and stooped as if some internal sickness was attacking him. His skin turned to the colour of the Autumn vine leaves and his eyes became dull like Folly's. When he visited he seemed to find it increasingly difficult to leave the Greenhouse. He spent hour upon hour just sitting inside.

Eventually his wife no longer accompanied him; he was lonely not for her but for Vanessa. He ached for her to materialize, but nothing more substantial than the lingering scent of her drifted on the air. He wished only to die here as his sister had, just to fall to the floor one intoxicating August afternoon and feed the vines. His desire for his own end hastened the decay within his body. He waited Summer after Summer for death, but his longing was not satisfied and each year he left more sadly for the city.

One year Hugo did not return; he had died in exile and was not buried in the churchyard beside Vanessa. His dearest wish remained unfulfilled.

When Thorne was informed of the news he became unsettled. He did not attend to his usual Autumn tasks. The apples were left to fall, bruise and rot where they lay, to be eaten greedily by woodmice and birds. It was their last glut of food before Winter. The doors of the Greenhouse were left open. Wasps came in multitudes to feed on the sweet juices of the grapes. Brambles grew unchecked so that they bore huge glistening fruits that dulled in October and gathered flies. No last crop was taken from the vegetable patch. Thorne had lost heart. His future and that of the Greenhouse were undetermined. There was no sign of Hugo's wife nor any indication of what she might decide to do. The Winter fluctuated between severe frost and mild Westerly winds that confused everything into premature growth. Shoots hung tattered from twigs, birds with dull feathers seemed unwilling to preen themselves in preparation for Spring. When those brightly lit, ever-changing days did finally come, the sight of the sun seemed only to point up more sharply the unkempt nature of the land.

It was not until July that everything recovered. The sun shone on the Greenhouse and its plants thrived. The vivid growth of all the flowers in the garden hid the weeds that increased at their feet. All that lived bred a new generation. Seeds and fruit were forming and ripening. Bees laden with nectar and pollen could hardly lift themselves out of the centres of flowers. A luscious fatness spread itself over all the land.

Thorne did not plant any vegetables that year.

Cars started to arrive at the house, singly at first. Thorne in his new role of caretaker would warily approach their occupants, ready to turn them away. The Greenhouse watched as they produced their credentials for the old gardener. Reluctantly he would acknowledge their right to be there, sullenly pull his bunch of keys from the pocket of his tweed coat and let the strangers into the house.

Shutters were partially drawn back and then closed as the intruders passed from room to room before emerging to examine the exterior of the house. On one occasion a man clambered over the double-pitched roof. On another two men walked the boundaries of the land, arriving finally at the Greenhouse. They pulled at its doors, rattling the catch, but it was locked and they were unable to step inside.

Instead they flattened their faces to its panes in an attempt to peer through, One of them noted something down on a clipboard before they left.

More and more cars came, carrying strangers. Thorne had almost a full-time job letting them into the house and locking up after them. They would walk the lawns, peer into borders and stand before the Greenhouse and discuss it, some admiring the beautiful old ironwork and carved stone, others terrifying the Greenhouse by planning how they would have it removed if they were to buy the property. The Greenhouse quickened with anxiety. As each new stranger pressed his face to its glass it recoiled. It was no longer able to notice the changes in the plants that grew inside it. Even Thorne was preoccupied and inattentive. Folly, by his side, would bristle and growl her mistrust at the visitors before slinking away to the yard. The Greenhouse thought of nothing else day or night but what was to be the outcome of all this alien activity.

One day a heavily laden lorry arrived, driving off the track and on to the lawn that separated the Greenhouse from the house. Inside it were four young men who jumped out and started to unload the back. One of them drilled deep holes in the lawn, into which they inserted tall poles of wood. Within an hour a huge white marquee had been erected in front of the Greenhouse. The men piled back into the lorry and were gone.

Thorne emerged with Folly. The dog sniffed about the guy ropes, wagging her tail at the new scents that she found. Thorne watched, the Greenhouse watched; they were both solemn with foreboding.

107

That night it rained. The wind got up, lashing the canvas of the tent, whistling through the ropes. An eerie noise like a distant moan haunted the Greenhouse, as if Vanessa were calling out across the lawns from the churchyard where she lay. It was a warning, a wail, for the loss that was due to take place when the day of the auction arrived and the house was to be plundered. The blank white wall moored before the Greenhouse swelled and slackened so that all about it became unstable. The Greenhouse longed for the wind to drop and the marquee to be calm, but it rippled and whispered its uneasy refrain all through the night, through the following day and the following night. The Greenhouse stood tormented and confused.

The nightmare reached its climax when the day came for the sale of the contents of the house. So many cars and vans arrived that the far lawn was used to park the vehicles that could not be accommodated on the track. The atmosphere was festive, as if some huge party were to be held at the house. A small van was sited on the gravel, from which cups of tea and coffee were dispensed to the intruders. Men in brown cotton coats had worked since the early morning, filling the inside of the marquee with the furniture that was to be sold.

Out of the house came a short, fat, red-faced man with thinnning, straw-coloured hair. He was wearing a tight tweed suit in spite of the heat: the auctioneer. He was followed into the tent by a tall blonde woman whom the Greenhouse recognized as Hugo's wife. She was smiling

108

graciously as if she were the hostess of this party receiving her guests. This was the day for which she had waited so many years. She was enjoying every detail of her separation from the house, the Greenhouse and the land for ever.

The auctioneer's hammer fell like an axe as he disposed of each lot. The Greenhouse recoiled from the blows. It felt as if one by one the trees of an ancient forest were being felled. The hammer struck on mahogany, walnut and oak. The torture continued throughout the day amidst constant activity as people carried away boxes filled with porcelain, silver and brass, dining chairs and gateleg tables, tallboys and wardrobes. Each item cared for by Vanessa and her family for generations was stripped of its identity, reduced to a number and a formal description in a catalogue. The pieces were loaded into vans, strapped awkwardly to the roofs of cars and finally driven away in convoy as if they were now the property of refugees leaving for another country.

At the end of the day the marquee was removed, leaving a bald rectangle on the grass as the only evidence of its presence. Litter blew about in the wind, lodged itself in flower beds, caught on the thorns of roses and floated away along the stream.

Throughout the night the wind buffeted against the Greenhouse, mimicking the beat of the auctioneer's hammer. Free to pass unhindered inside the house, it echoed in empty rooms, whistled through the joists of uncarpeted floors, forced its way down chimneys into hearths stripped of fender and fire iron, fingered the patches on walls where paintings had hung, gathered the dusty detritus of the past into heaps before abandoning it and escaping through undraped windows into the wood.

The second day came: the day of the auction of the house and its land, the farm and its land, the farm equipment and the livestock. Once again the auctioneer arrived closely followed by Hugo's wife, who was eager to witness every last memory and association severed. The Greenhouse heard the hammer fall. Its fate was determined.

Throughout the sale Thorne and Folly were nowhere to be seen. They had hidden themselves away behind the Greenhouse wall. Thorne's future too had been resolved; he had come to his own decision about what he would do when the house was sold. To witness the lengthy details of the transactions taking place would have been too painful for the old man. The Greenhouse wished that it could have removed to the other side of the wall as well, so as not to have seen and heard as, lot by lot, everything was taken away.

When the last shed had been emptied, the contents of the last cupboard, and indeed the cupboard itself, sold, the vandals all left except for Hugo's wife. She remained for a while inside the house, closing shutters. The Greenhouse listened to the sound of her footsteps echoing across bare floorboards, resonating against the walls and corners of the rooms. Finally she locked the front door and came down the steps, but as she was about to get into her car she hesitated, turned, and made her way to the Greenhouse.

It waited for her, waited for her to enter, but as always on reaching the long-grassed bank, she stopped. The

Greenhouse was a force that lay beyond her understanding. The savage regenerative power of nature emanated from it, throbbed behind its glass eyes that stared out blankly, reflecting the sky. Always it had looked down at her from its height. Now she neither understood nor cared, for on this afternoon she had been freed from it for ever. All that terrible green growth and obsession of Vanessa's and Hugo's had been turned into the only thing that really meant anything to her: money. She hoped that someone like herself had bought the property and would tame it; that they would order the flowerbeds, curb the excessive growth of the climbing plants and demolish the Greenhouse, that they would raze the vines that sucked on blood and relentlessly produced their swollen fruits, and so destroy its inaccessible, mystical, inner life. She cursed the plants that continually blossomed and sprouted, springing up in places where they were unwanted; they strangled their own and were blemished by insects and decay.

She looked over to the churchyard, to where Vanessa and Edgar were buried under the yew. Its acid underlay was so poisonous that even if the twin-winged seeds of the fertile sycamore were to germinate, then one would die instantly while the other uncurled its root only to perish. In the field beyond, the dung beetle burrowed into the excrement of a cow, the maggot bored through the ripe flesh of an apple and the carrion crow picked at the eyes of a dying sheep.

The Greenhouse glittered brightly in the sunlight. Hugo's wife was awed by it. To her it was an unholy vision, and she raised her hand and crossed herself. She was afraid

111

of it and needed this sign to protect herself from her own incomprehension. Hugo's widow turned her back on the Greenhouse for the last time and walked to her car. Thorne was holding open the door. She exchanged a few words with him, handed him a large, long white envelope and left.

No-one came for several weeks. Thorne emerged from his retreat and began to work once again in the garden. The leaves of the trees changed colour and fierce spirals of Autumn wind ripped them from their branches.

During one long solitary night the Greenhouse heard a rustle outside the doors, one of which now hung off its hinges. Startled, it strained to listen, and tensed with alarm as something moved stealthily between the ivy and brambles, startling birds on their roosts. Two green moons of eyes entered through the small gap in the Greenhouse door and slid silently into its interior. The shadow, the stain, the foetid mould was once again inside. Powerless to stop it the Greenhouse felt it thread its way amongst the growth at its floor. It slunk behind the vines. Silence. Nothing moved, no bird nor bat; the insects clasped their wings to their bodies. The warm shadow crouched motionless between the vines. The Greenhouse waited, waited, waited for what it knew was to happen. The scream of a pheasant savaged where it sat fixed by fear to the ground. It got up in a wounded flurry of feathers and fell back on to the tiles. The shadow struck again at the broken bird. The kill. The fox left with the bird clasped tight between its jaws. Blood dripped across the floor and on to the earth at the roots of the vines. The Greenhouse felt a breeze like an exhalation of breath pass through its interior.

The grapes on the vines ripened, but in the close shade they were damp. The unthinned bunches grew taut, and as each fruit swelled it crushed in upon itself, until the tension split its skin. They were raided by swarms of wasps that sucked the juice from their sweet flesh. The inside of the Greenhouse was filled with the buzzing of insects and it longed each night for a keen frost so that they would return to their nests and leave it in peace. As each fruit was damaged it turned brown and shrivelled. On the decay grey mould began to form, rapidly spreading its furred tentacles over the surface of the grapes, clasping each in a long-fingered fist of putrefaction that tightened its grip in the humid Autumn air. With the rot came the acrid smell of grapes fermenting that always reminded the Greenhouse of Vanessa and the harvest ritual.

One day in early December the Greenhouse watched Thorne down by the stream, clearing the reeds just as he had done on the first day he had come to work for Vanessa. In between filling the wheelbarrow he paused for a while and gazed down into the water. The Greenhouse was comforted to see that the old grey heron had returned. Folly was by his side, arthritic but still devoted and alert. The low rays of the Winter sunlight threw the man and his dog into relief against the Eastern sky and the withered yellow grass of the water meadow. For an instant they were frozen, a flawless scrap of memory. Then Thorne stooped down to pick up a small bundle that lay beside him on the bank. From it he took a length of twine, made a loop at one end passed the other about the neck of the dog. Thorne's actions were surprising, for the Greenhouse had never seen Folly on a lead before. The old dog was well trained and would always walk closely to heel. Her entire life had been spent within the boundaries of the farmyard and the grounds. Thorne had never taken her with him to the village when he returned there at night. He would feed her and then chain her to her barrel, where she slept until the following day, emerging each morning for him to release her.

Still holding on to one end of the string, Thorne led her beside the barrow slowly back towards the Greenhouse. His face was passive with sadness. Thorne stopped in front of the Greenhouse and raised his cap in acknowledgement before continuing across the lawn to the back of the house. The Greenhouse watched a drift of smoke rise between the bare twigs of the elm. Thorne had made a bonfire of the debris that he had collected from the stream. Just before dusk he reappeared from behind the house, Folly still tied to him by the piece of string, the small bundle clasped under his arm. The old man and the dog walked slowly away in the direction of the lime trees. The Greenhouse wanted to cry out to stop them; it realized that Thorne was leaving for ever to walk the lanes with Folly so that nothing he loved could ever be taken from him again. The Greenhouse ached at the loss as it watched the two frail old creatures until they were finally swallowed up by the wood. If the Greenhouse could have sobbed for the loneliness that it felt, if it could have extracted the wedge of pain that was lodged in its interior, if it could have expressed its grief at this final blow, it would have done. But it had to remain bolted to its wall and endure all that was to happen until the end.

After Thorne and Folly had left it was as if the landscape was made of granite. The frosts were bitter and shattered several panes of glass, causing a deep chill inside the Greenhouse that numbed its pain. It stood quite alone, glass eyes staring, bereft of all hope. The frosts were followed by snow. It fell in such quantities that flakes found their way between gaps in the glass and floated silently down on to the Greenhouse's tiled floor. Outside it built up inch by inch and was drifted by the wind, piled into banks that smothered the ground, blanketing everything in a cold security.

Loneliness became familiar: a faint chill at night that evaporated at dawn. The snow stayed well into the Spring. Early snowdrops and daffodils fought to find the light, scattering their blooms above the frozen crystal surface of the earth. A blackbird died in a tangle of paper-dry undergrowth in its fruitless search for something to eat. Every plant had been stripped of berries; every patch of ground that lay uncovered, scoured. The bark on every tree, the crack in every wall, had been searched for anything that might provide some relief to the dreadful hunger of the countryside. All creatures became silent and grim in their pursuit. Even the robin hardly sang; he just perched, his throat drawn back into his body, and watched with a hard black eye for some change, some reprieve from the endless Winter. By April the snow had melted until only traces of it could be seen against tufts of couch grass in the meadow, or beneath the shadowed wall of the house.

Untended, the garden grew. The lawns became meadows, the stream was clogged with reeds. Brambles thickened and increased with the ivy up the low walls of the Greenhouse until they reached the glass, scrambled upwards into gutters and twisted through fretwork until before long the Greenhouse was almost entirely hidden from sight.

Living its secret life the Greenhouse became secure, protected by its tangled mantle against frosts and kept cool from the hottest rays of the midday sun. The vines still flourished, acclimatizing themselves to the cooler conditions and the lack of care. Unpruned, they grew freely to the height of the Greenhouse. Their lateral shoots thickened until they formed a skeletal structure that supported it from within. As slowly each wooden rib decayed it was replaced by a thick branch of vine, whose roots still fed on Vanessa's and Edgar's blood. Only the lilies suffered. Those that did not stand under broken panes of glass became parched, and their scaly bulbs shrivelled. But each Summer there were still a few extraordinary blooms to scent the interior. Small creatures had long ago started to inhabit the Greenhouse. Thrushes and wrens chose nest sites under the glass and in the ivy that grew up outside, so that from dawn to dusk the air was filled with constant birdsong. Fieldmice and voles burrowed about the roots of the vines, in piles of raffia and straw that they collected from where Thorne had laid them over the lilies before he left. Insects of all descriptions took over, finding in the rotting ribs of the Greenhouse a multitude of hiding places. Lacewings and ladybirds clustered in the corners of the glass panes, tight against the wood and were disturbed only by the tortoiseshell butterflies that emerged prematurely from hibernation whenever the slightest ray of sunlight warmed their frozen veins, releasing the bronze glory of their patterned wings before they were destroyed by the cold Spring air. Spiders slung webs between anything that would support them and patiently sat, cradled in their dusty hammocks. Earwigs raised their anaemic young in the chambers of the old, dry seedpods of the lilies. Primitive-looking armoured woodlice gorged away their lives in secrecy on the underside of rotting wood. Worms passed the decay at the foot of the vines through their red bodies and returned their fertile excrement to the earth.

The water tap over the tank outside the Greenhouse still hissed in Summer and froze in Winter. No-one disturbed the Greenhouse, but the children in the village knew of its whereabouts. Stories of the vines and their sinister crop of grapes were told and elaborated by one child after another. Tales of the mother and son whose unhappy lives had ended within the Greenhouse were woven together into impossible tangled fables, and grew like an untamed briar in a hedgerow and festered in their minds like fungus on a once proud tree. A whisper spread amongst the children

117

that those who would not enter the Greenhouse and eat the grapes that fed on human blood were cowards.

The Greenhouse heard the sound of something approaching and was afraid that it was the fox returning for another kill. A waxing moon was beginning to rise through low cloud and mist. Huge and pale in the moist night air, it bulged and strained in its half-finished form as if with one single thrust it could become full and ripe. The noise came closer, the rushing watery sound of something travelling through damp grass. The dry hollow stems of the tall hemlock and cow parsley cracked as they were parted by not one figure moving towards the Greenhouse but several. Seeing that they were dwarfed by the vegetation the Greenhouse realized that they were children.

Each of them carried a stick with which to beat at the undergrowth as they crossed what used to be the lawn, stumbling forward in the dark against the bindweed and the sharp-bladed couch grass. The leader carried a torch and, on reaching the higher ground, directed them to stop where they stood. He turned round, faced the group and whispered for one to come forward. The moon escaped from the cloud and its light caught the fair hair of a small girl as she was pushed to the front of the line. The Greenhouse watched as she was shoved up the bank, parting the nettles with her bare hands until she reached the steps, where she stopped as if reluctant to go further. The older boy jabbed his torch into her back, bullying the girl, taunting her for her timidity. The others huddled

118

together in the moonlight, immobilized, while the nettles pumped the contents of their acid poison sacs into bare legs. High above their heads rose the enormous shadowy Greenhouse, a huge sleeping monster covered with ivy whose waxy leaves snapped against one another as the wind whistled through it, weaving in and out of the broken panes of glass. The fair-haired girl pulled at the block of wood that now held fast one of the doors; eerily it swung open, grating on its unoiled hinge. The children stood stock-still looking into the dark, cavernous depths. The Greenhouse sucked in the cold night air and waited. Small birds clung rigidly to their roosts, feathers taut and sleek in preparation for flight, cries of alarm choked in their throats.

A vixen screamed; her bloodcurdling cry terrified the expectant children. One by one they followed the torch up the steps and into the Greenhouse. Inside, they stumbled on the broken stone that once composed the Greenhouse's intricately patterned floor. The gnarled roots of the vines had strained upwards as they had grown and cracked the tiles into a sea of broken terracotta. Cobwebs stuck to their faces; brambles and the curled tendrils of the vines caught at their clothes, wrapped themselves around ankles. They stood transfixed as the torch shone upwards on to the grapes that fed on blood. Sick with fear the children waited for a command. A thousand bright eyes watched from their hiding places. In every crevice, behind every leaf, a creature lurked and waited in silence, on the defensive. The Greenhouse watched; its last few glass eyes reflected the core of the torch's beam. Outside, the dog fox barked in reply to the vixen. Terrified, the boys and girls leapt and tore at the grapes. The partially rotting clusters burst in their scrabbling fingers. Mould travelled through the air in clouds. Birds, unsettled from their roosts, flew at them screaming before thudding against the ribs of the Greenhouse. Butterflies opened and closed their wings. Ladybirds and lacewings made jumpy flights to more remote corners. Spiders plummeted on threads towards the ground, there to scuttle into corners and wrap their legs about their bodies. The Greenhouse reverberated with the triumphant cries of the children as each seized his own prize of a bunch of grapes. It felt the heat of their breath and the warmth of their bodies; the atmosphere was charged with fear. They believed that it was blood that they drank as they placed the grapes inside their mouths and burst them between their teeth, licking and sucking at the juice that flowed down their faces before it splattered on to the floor and was trampled underfoot. The boy dropped his torch, its bulb broke and it rolled away out of reach. Plunged into absolute dark, they began to make for the doors. Tripping and falling down the steps, the children fled into the moonlight, stumbling through the night.

From inside the Greenhouse came an inhuman cry. It chilled the air, froze time; a cry as bleak as a great loss; a cry as distant as a continent; a cry that withered even the echo of the wind; a cry of madness, of despair.

It started to rain and the Greenhouse, alone with its own misery, felt the water slide from one lead to another and drip on to the floor. The half-formed moon emerged small and sharp between the clouds, flattening the mist with its icy bright stare, piercing the inner recesses of the Greenhouse.

For the entire night the Greenhouse endured the agitated rustlings of birds and insects returning to the safety of their former refuges. The rain came intermittently, and the accumulated water on the floor swept the juice of the torn grapes towards the roots of the vines. They fed upon themselves, just as the trees in the wood sucked on their own detritus. Just before dawn the vixen and the dog fox mated. Silence smothered the land.

It was an unusual Autumn. The Greenhouse lived in a sharp crystalline world. Hoar frosts extended every leaf on every tree, every blade of grass, fringed them with ice, leaving only their green hearts open to the sun. Day after day the crystals grew more pointed and complex, but in the depths of the Greenhouse the air remained temperate. Nothing penetrated its decay. It was as if a warm heart throbbed within its frame, sustaining those few degrees between life and death.

Summer came and sunlight filtered through to the leaves of the vines in pale green shafts, rested like dew on all that it touched, breathed life into the plants that grew on the floor of the Greenhouse. Huge white lilies shone pale as the moon, their scent as thick as the growth that surrounded them. When soft rain fell on midsummer evenings, filling the air with the mixture of freshness and decay that the warmth of such rain brings, the Greenhouse would look out on the brightness of the dripping leaves on the trees, listen to the last song and call of the hidden bird, followed by the sodden silence, watch until the shadows merged with the viridian of the trees and the creatures of the night emerged, lustrous-eyed and silk-footed, from the depths of the undergrowth.

One morning the Greenhouse heard the noise of a tractor coming up the lime avenue. It strained to see out through its last topmost panes. The tractor was followed by an open-backed truck filled with sacks and ladders. Both vehicles stopped in front of the house. Several men got out of the truck and went in through the front door. Throughout the day load upon load of plaster and wood were carried out by the team of men and piled into the truck. Long ladders were placed against the outside walls and a cage of scaffolding was erected. Men crawled over the roof, hung out of windows, ran up and down the scaffolding. Even through the tangle of growth that now separated the Greenhouse from the world it could hear the grating of a saw upon wood, the mechanical whirr of an electric drill, the sounds of hammer, chisel and plane. Tirelessly those men worked as the weeks went by, tearing away at the ancient skeleton of the house, stripping it of its past.

The men left. The cage had gone. The house stood as bright and new as the day that it was built. Only the garden was still in a state of decay.

*

The Summer growth had almost covered every last pane of the Greenhouse. It was entirely smothered by a huge mound of vegetation, which formed a hill against its retaining wall.

Inside, the birds nested and their squabs squawked for food. Insects sucked on leaves and the bodies of aphids. The plants transpired with health. Outside the fox and the owl and the magpie fed on the fat of the new-born.

The tractor that had stood for so long outside the house was moved down to the water meadow where it began to plough. The Greenhouse watched all day as it ran backwards and forwards following the line of the wood. It moved closer and closer until by sunset it had reached the boundary of the stream. There it stopped. All through the night the Greenhouse could smell the newly turned earth. The roots of upturned yellow buttercup, white dog daisy, pink campion, blue cranesbill and creamy scented meadowsweet sucked in the moisture of the night air in a futile attempt to live until the sun rose and parched them to their deaths.

The tractor crossed the bridge, its huge metal swipe trailing behind. It started work along the near bank of the stream, up and down, backwards and forwards it moved, on and on across the old lawns. Grass, cow parsley and hemlock were smashed to broken straws. Fieldmice and voles scuttled for cover only to be flayed to death to the sound of the clamouring chain. The fox hid behind the churchyard wall. Night fell and the destruction ceased. The fox emerged and gnawed on the ready slain flesh of a rabbit.

The Greenhouse, the vines, and the ivy that hung over them clung together throughout the night, waiting for dawn.

The following morning an immense red machine with a great claw at the front came up the avenue. It stopped in front of the house, turned, and approached on huge rubber tracks across the lawn, leaving rough scars in the grass. It rose up the banks between the stumps of briar, twisted and manoeuvred until it was in line with the Greenhouse.

It drew back, lowering its claw, and drove directly towards the Greenhouse, scouring the earth. The Greenhouse looked down into the gaping red jaws. Deafened by the noise, it watched. The claw approached, struck the steps, metal on stone. It withdrew gasping, its oily blood running faster, and shifted into another gear. It staggered on the bank before returning, claw raised high in the air. It struck. Iron filled its metal teeth as it withdrew, dragging part of the Greenhouse with it.

It came again and hit the stone pillars. They crumbled their satin dust on the ground. Still the iron columns supported the Greenhouse, rising high into the tangled mass of iron and wood. The man-made jaws spat out the debris. The earth outside was now so deeply furrowed that the machine tipped and slithered in the bald wet clay. Screaming as it slid forward through the great gash that it had made, churning and cutting at the roots of the vines as it entered the Greenhouse, it raised its fist upwards, shattering every single pane of glass, and showered splinters

against the sun. They exploded into a rainbow of minute
fragments.

The machine stopped. Total silence. Clouds formed tight
about the sun so that it could not hear the terrible cry of
the Greenhouse as it fell to the earth.